WOLVES' GOLD

WOLVES CLOUD

WOLVES' GOLD
A WESTERN DOUBLE

LEVI JOHNSON MOUNTAIN MAN SCOUT
BOOK THREE

ASH LINGAM

WOLFPACK
PUBLISHING
— EST 2013 —

Wolves' Gold
Paperback Edition
Copyright © 2025 (As Revised) by Ash Lingam

Wolfpack Publishing
1707 E. Diana Street
Tampa, Florida 33610

www.wolfpackpublishing.com

Paperback ISBN 979-8-89567-232-7
Ebook ISBN 979-8-89567-231-0

CONTENTS

CONTENTS

WOLVES' GOLD

WOLVES' GOLD

LEVI JOHNSON MOUNTAIN MAN
SCOUT 5

This book is dedicated to Stinky the Dog.

The measure of intelligence is the ability to change.

Albert Einstein

STRANGERS

LEVI BEAVER JOHNSON AND EX-ARMY CAPTAIN WILL Forrester went hunting like they had been doing for several days. The first light frost had hit the Rocky Mountains, so it was easy to see footprints in the crushed grass. Two mules trailed the pair as they carefully walked their horses through the woods. The frost crinkled as it crumbled under foot and hoof. Their breaths were visible in the crisp early morning air. A thick mist appeared in patches of the woods. One moment they could see, and the next, visibility was not more than a couple of yards before their faces.

They had set out anew an hour before first light to catch animals seeking someplace to quench their thirst. If you were careful and didn't make any noise, some wild game usually would risk the chance and take a drink. Levi already knew where every water hole was within twenty miles of the cabins. The rest of the men in the compound were preparing the traps for the coming season. They had over fifty sets of iron jaws to inspect. It wouldn't do for a trap to malfunction and the beaver to get away. The pelts were too valuable to let them escape, especially with there being fewer and fewer every season. On the good side, this fact increased the prices.

The gunshot made Levi's ears ring. Like always, his bullet hit its mark. The elk dropped, and its legs folded like a house of cards. Forrester hadn't even seen the animal, but Levi had already taken a bead. They climbed astride their horses and gigged them into a trot, riding toward the kill. They kept their eyes on their surroundings. They may not have been the only ones to have heard the gunshot.

As they rode over the rise just past the dead buck elk, they saw prints in the frosty grass—lots of tracks. The strange thing about it was that they were heading up the mountain and not down. Levi wheeled his horse around but saw nobody. He closed his eyes and breathed in deeply. He thought he smelled sweat, but it was so faint he wasn't sure.

"Who would be fool enough to climb any farther into the mountains at summer's end?" Levi asked.

"You know more about such things than I do," Forrester replied. "I think it could be just about anybody."

"I hope it ain't more buffalo hunters," Levi huffed. "We've had enough trouble with that bunch of scoundrels already. They draw Indians like horses draw flies."

Johnson kicked his leg over the pummel and slid off his horse. Ice crunched under his feet. He kneeled and looked closely at the footprints.

"Men, horses, and mules," Levi said as he looked up the trail. "There must be a dozen, but there's something that don't make sense." He stood, moved off the trampled trail a few yards more, and then stopped again. "Wolves, too. It's a big pack. I reckon they passed after the strangers. Let's follow 'im when we finish guttin' and skinnin' the elk. Maybe we can see what's up from afar, so they don't know we're here. I got my spyglass right here." He patted his shirt.

He studied the tracks some more and said, "That's strange."

"What's strange now? Can't we ever go on a peaceful hunt?" Forrester asked. He just knew something was going to ruin their day.

"They didn't all pass this way at the same time," Levi replied, puzzled. "It looks like they were broken up into small groups. Now it makes less sense than before. If they're in ones and twos, they'll have the hungry wolves trackin' 'em too, not to mention the Indians. I reckon the animals feel the shortage of wild game just like us."

"How in the world can you tell that?" Forrester asked. "How do you know they're in groups rather than together? Have you become a mystic too?"

"Some of the first frost has melted more in some footprints than others. I reckon they were either followed or followin', all headin' the easiest path up. Whoever they are, the mules are loaded down. I can tell by the way they drag their hooves. They ain't happy animals."

"Let's gut and skin this elk and cut him up and follow the tracks," Forrester said. "Lately, everybody that comes up here unannounced seems to bring trouble. Maybe we can stop it before it starts."

By the time they were done, the frost on the ground had thawed and turned to mud. The tracks of the strangers were still easy to follow, though. They seemed to all be heading to the same place. The mountain men wondered where and what that was. Overhead, six vultures lazily circled, waiting for the hunters to finish. Strings of crows sat on branches squawking and cawing as they waited to start the feast. Soon the coyotes would arrive; then it would be a feeding frenzy. There was plenty of the elk left to satisfy a few scavengers.

They saddled up, each man with a mule's lead in hand. They walked the horses along the edge of the woods where open stretches of land used to be occupied by buffalo. Now, the grass grew long.

"It looks like the buffalo ain't been by these parts this year," Levi said as he watched the grass blow in the wind.

"How do you know?" Will asked. "Sometimes I feel stupid compared to you. At least in the wilderness." He looked at his friend with narrowed eyes and a tiny smile.

"Otherwise, the grass would be eaten to the nub." Levi laughed. "You ain't dumb by a long sight, but you lack the basic knowledge of the wilderness—how everything feeds off each other. It's the chain of Mother Nature. It must be a vicious life out here for any animal but a grizzly. Even then, they fight each other for territory or females. Imagine having your life with such challenges every day."

"We aren't that far off the wild animals' situations," Will said. "If things stay like they have since we left Kansas, my expectations for something good are low to nonexistent."

"The only difference is we have weapons to fight 'em

off," Levi said. "Some grizzlies ya can't even kill with a rifle. They swat at bullets like they're flies."

"I'd rather run into a Comanche than a grizzly bear," Will said.

"How's that arm healing up on ya, pard?" Levi asked. "You never talk about it anymore."

"That's because there's nothin' to talk about," Will said, locking eyes with his friend. "I really don't think about it anymore." He looked down at his empty sleeve.

"Let's go see what's goin' on," Levi said and gigged his horse, breaking into at trot. His mule, Dot, protested but followed just the same. "I wanna see what it is before Rusty gets wind of whatever's goin' on."

Forrester spurred his white stallion, which shot off like its hair was on fire, leaving Levi's horse, Tac, and Dot in his dust. He left his mule to follow Levi—it ran after them like a puppy. Johnson just shook his head and continued to follow carefully, watching the track for direction changes or someone breaking off and circling around. Then they would be behind him. Since he didn't know what he was dealing with, he had to expect the worst. Maybe some wanted outlaws had come up to the mountain to hide out for the winter.

Rusty Steel had said it happened in the past but not for some time. He claimed they showed up like cockroaches out of a fire for a while. Somebody figured they could hide out up in the Rockies. They obviously didn't think it through. That winter, over twenty outlaws came to the mountains to hide out. They did hide from the law well enough, but they weren't prepared for what they encountered, and they perished, to the last man, that first winter. Traces of some were never even found.

Maybe they got eaten and dragged away by a grizzly or pack of wolves.

Of course, it wasn't just the animals, because there were also a half dozen hostile Indian tribes within riding distance in pretty much any direction you went. All these Indians had only one thing in common—their hatred for the White race. Many attacked any whites they encountered unless it was too dangerous. Indians were smart like that. They would reconsider the attack if they stood to lose too many warriors, unlike White men, who throw bodies at their enemies like meat grinders. The depletion of the enemy's ammunition was an Army officer's primary objective.

Since you could never be sure in the wilderness, Levi continued with caution. He watched as Will and his white horse disappeared into a stand of young trees. Levi was on alert but not paranoid. He doubted anyone could catch him, although he could get bushwhacked from a distance if they were a good shot. But he was confident in his skills. They stemmed from his childhood. His family had lived in the wilderness of southwest Indiana, and he'd trapped and hunted all his life. Unlike the captain, a West Point graduate who was disgraced by losing half of his expedition west to locate places to build new Army forts. Then he lost his arm.

He pulled out his spyglass and scoured the mountains surrounding him. He traced across the ridges looking for silhouettes. He caught sight of a flash in the far distance. Even too far ahead for the spy glass to see it clearly. Then it flashed again soon after Forrester returned. He was too nervous, and his horse was worse than him. The stallion stomped its hooves in anticipation of breaking into a run again.

"Did ya see that?" Levi asked.

Forrester nodded. "Yeah, that even I could spot—especially since it flashed twice. I saw it from out front too. It could be the chrome of a weapon or some tool. Or a spyglass like yours."

"That's what I figured," Levi said. "Maybe even a mirror some fool's using. They're well ahead of us, but we'll catch up. Hopefully, they ain't in a hurry to get wherever they're goin'."

"And where in the world could that be?" Forrester asked. "The farther you go up this mountain, the harder going it gets. We've only made it to where we would have to leave the mules behind. Wherever it is, it'll be before that. This trail goes all the way to the top, but it's impossible to do with horses, although the mules may be surefooted enough to get at least part way up."

"With the pack-mules loaded down like that, I'm sure they won't leave 'em behind. They won't be able to carry their load. They've got somethin' worth lugging all the way up here, so they'll have to stop about halfway between here and the top."

As midday arrived, the sun bore down and dried the dirt into a cloud of crusty dust that corkscrewed behind the mules and horses. They pressed the animals, or they would never catch up. They knew they wouldn't be back today, but that was common enough when they went hunting. Anyway their curiosity was too intense for them to turn around, and they felt it their duty to those in the compound to follow any intruders and find out why they were there.

It wasn't until the sun blushed rose on the horizon that they saw silhouettes on the ridges in the last rays of light. There were a couple of stragglers. About a mile's distance separated them. Finally, they disappeared over the mountain as the sun vanished behind them. Levi wondered precisely where they were going and who they were.

They hobbled their horses and mules and waited until the half-moon rose, providing enough light to continue on foot. If they led the way, they could avoid injuring one of the animals, but at the same time, continue in their pursuit. Still, they didn't know who they were following or what they were doing.

As they rode up steep grades in the trail, Forrester whispered, "What if it's the Army?"

"What in the world would the Army be doing way up here?" Levi asked. "You don't think you're such a big deal that they'll come to fetch ya back, do ya? Somebody would know it's too dodgy to climb up too high this time of year. A freak blizzard could cost the lives of a patrol, plus you boys never traveled so disorganized. You'd have your men altogether and in a straight line with their chins held high. Before we hit the Comanche, you and your boys looked to be as fine a cavalry as the Army had. I don't see these stragglers being soldiers with the way they ride."

It was time for the weather to change. Already, some days were chilly, although others were still warm. But when the temperatures plummeted at night, it got cold enough to leave a thin layer of ice on top of the water barrels and watering troughs.

"I figure we'll find the stragglers before first light iffin they kept a fire goin' to ward off the chill," Levi said. "We'll be able to smell the smoke, which will lead us to their camp. Once we're close, we'll see the fire."

"What do we do when we get there?" Will asked.

"I guess we'll find out in the mornin'." Levi smiled. "I suppose it all depends on what we see and who we think they might be."

As they traveled through the night, they kept their ears trained on animal sounds. Things like owls and coyotes were always suspect. The Indians expertly mimicked both, along with a variety of birds. Levi could always tell the real ones from the Indians making bird calls, though. They felt different to him. As he spent more time in the Rockies, he sensed he was peeling away any trace of modernization and civilization like the layers of an onion. He felt like he was becoming the essence of man, like when the Plains Indians roamed this country before White men even set foot on the American Continent.

He suddenly stopped in mid-stride. "Can ya smell it?" Levi whispered.

Forrester stopped, sniffed the air and smiled. "Yeah, we must be close if I smell it too."

"I think it'll be in the next clearing. I was hoping they would camp more in the open, but we're going to have to get close. How are you at sneakin' up on folks with the one arm?"

"I lost an arm, not a leg," he spat and shot a look at Levi that would peel paint off a wall.

It was clear Capt. Will Forrester didn't want anybody to make exceptions for him or baby him due to the loss of his right arm, even though he was right-handed. He preferred to ignore his handicap and trudge on like nothing had happened. The man had more grit than most, that was for sure. Since he was obviously touchy on the issue, Levi felt better, and he left the subject. He was proud of his friend anyway. Just the way he acted made all the men in the compound see the courage in the blemished Army captain.

Levi strapped his rifle over his shoulder and said, "Well, let's get to it. We're gonna have to crawl up on 'em. Cut some leaves and branches and stick 'em in your hair. It'll make us harder to see. I learned that from that Sioux Indian that was spyin' on us a while back. I admit they be clever rascals."

Levi was catching on very quickly. He learned all he could from the mountain men back at the cabins, especially Rusty Steel and Mountain Dennis. But he learned even more from the Indians. Even when they fought, it unlocked secrets that he absorbed like a sponge. With every confrontation, he felt more like he knew what they would do. Nothing about nature and the locals got past the young mountain man.

The two hunters crawled through the dark, between short stubby trees with lots of leaves rustling in the breeze. Soon, they smelled coffee as it danced on puffs of air. A man was sitting on a rock with a shotgun in his hands, keeping watch on the horses. Burlap sacks lay in stacks beside their camp between them and the hobbled horses. The double-barrel had a shortened stock, so it was more of a scattergun. It is not very effective at a distance, but at close range, it could shoot lead pellets into a man from head to toe. The hunters exchanged glances and silently wiggled their way into some bushes so they wouldn't be seen when the sun came up.

The man on the rock didn't seem to be sleepy or nervous. Levi could smell his sweet tobacco and see the glow of the bowl on the smoker's face. Little by little, the horizon began to lighten as the sun climbed its way up the other side of the world. Eventually, an eye peeked over the earth's end and shot rays of light across the country, slaying the night for another day.

They immediately saw the picks, shovels, and miners' wash pans. The men wore long beards and hair, and much of it was gray or even white. It looked like a strange assortment of men, but their purpose was unmistakable.

"They must be miners," Levi mouthed to Will, and he nodded back.

Levi tossed his head to one side and backed out as Will followed. When they were a safe distance away, they stood and ran for the horses far enough away that if one nickered, it wouldn't be heard.

"They ain't nothing but miners," Levi said, confused.

"But there's no gold up here," Forrester said, puzzled. "If there were gold, the military would know about it and use it to draw even more people west. Nobody has ever found gold in the Rocky Mountains, as far as I know."

"Well, what are we gonna do?" Levi asked. "We might as well go have a jaw-wag with 'em. Maybe we can find out where all this gold is or whatever they're after. Miners look for silver, gold, and turquoise, as far as I know, and there's never been any found in the Rockies. After over ten years, Dennis would have come across it were it here."

"You can't say for sure that there's no gold in all the Rocky Mountains," Forrester corrected him. "We don't know everything about these mountains. They are so vast that most have never been seen by anybody but the Indians. I believe only they would know every square foot of the mountains. Even the peaks."

"If there was gold, the Indians that lived here for the last ten thousand years would know, and I never heard any tales about such a thing," Levi said and laughed. "They must be plum crazy if that's what they're after. If we don't question 'em, Rusty will just come up here and do it himself, and he might not be so friendly."

"The word you want is diplomatic." Forrester laughed. "You know, with Rusty Steel, diplomacy will go right out the window the minute he sees strangers on the mountain. I get the feeling the boys think it's theirs. I wonder who it really belongs to. I don't mean on paper, either. We know Washington thinks they own all the land even though nobody's been here to survey."

"I don't want any more trouble from nobody," Levi said. "There's been enough blood shed on this mountain. Sometimes I don't know where it's more dangerous, back in the big Eastern cities or out here in the mountains."

"I guess it all depends on the city," Forrester said.

UNWELCOME VISIT

WHEN LEVI AND FORRESTER RETURNED TO THE compound, they got the surprise of their lives. On the porch were Rusty Steel and Angus McFarlin yelling at three men who appeared to be miners. They could hear him yell well before they had the compound in sight. You would think the Comanche were attacking them again. The two brought their horses into a quick trot as they closed in on the compound, just in case they needed help.

"Can you believe this?" Rusty asked, beside himself. He turned to the two men riding in. "Can you believe these fools are climbing all over our mountain lookin' for gold when there's never been a single nugget found in the Rockies in all the years White men have been snooping around and thousands of years for the Indians?"

Levi pulled to a stop, unsure how to drop the news on him when he was already upset, but maybe it was best. He doubted Rusty could get much angrier. A man can only get so mad.

"We found a dozen more miners climbin' up the mountain," Levi said. "Folks pretty much like them."

"And what did they tell you as to why they think there's gold in them hills?" Rusty asked. "This fool said somebody told him they read it somewhere, but since he can't read himself, he didn't get any details. Can you believe a man gives up everything to follow a lie that somebody might have said?"

"It's because they saw it printed in the newspaper in Old Fort Boise. It supposedly said a fella struck it filthy rich up here," Levi said, explaining what he'd been told. "The rag said this fella found the mother lode, but the miners we talked to told us the article didn't mention the man's name, nor did they say exactly where in the Rocky Mountains the discovery was. Of course, every fool who read it figured it was a lifetime opportunity. Don't they know they'll die up here if the weather turns?"

"They've got the gold fever," Rusty said. "They won't care about nothing until they end up dead, one way or another. If there was gold up here, don't you think Dennis, Angus, or I would know about it? It's all a load of hogwash. When we first came here, all of us spent a spell lookin' for gold or silver just in case, but when we came up dry one after the other, we all gave it up. There's no sense lookin' for somethin' that ain't there, and only a fool believes a newspaper article with so little information on the details. Heck, there aren't any details."

"I've heard of the Army doin' such things to encourage people west to populate the land even though they knew there never was any gold in the first place," Forrester said. "I know many things the Army did to the Indians that you wouldn't believe."

"All they wanna do is encourage people to come and push the Indians off their land," Levi said. "Boy-oh-boy, are the Crow gonna get all riled up when they see all these miners runnin' around. I reckon there'll be a scalp or three taken. We also saw lots of tracks of a big pack of wolves—I mean, massive. I ain't ever seen nothin' like it. We've only seen the tracks so far, but I doubt they'll take long to do something that will draw our attention."

"That's because all these people keep comin' up here and killing all the game and trappin' out the creeks and streams of beaver," Angus spat. "The same thing is happening to the buffalo. What was sixty million might not be more than six million now, and they're still dwindling."

"The Army backs that too," Forrester said.

The captain was developing a grudge against his old employer. Maybe it had something to do with the loss of his arm, who knew, but he seemed to complain and disclose violent acts from the Army more than before.

"You know the Army's important, and without it, our country wouldn't exist and would be defenseless against our enemies," Levi said. "The problem is, they treat the Indians like some third-class nomads and only look for ways to eliminate 'em. Nobody even treats them like human beings."

"Now we're gonna have to keep our heads down," Angus said. "I reckon we have almost enough meat for the winter, and we're stocked up on beans. It may not be safe to go huntin' for a spell. It won't just be the Indians after the miners. That pack of wolves may well follow 'em and all. The tracks run right behind 'em, so they're stalking 'em all right. Iffin they leave too many scraps, the wolves may get brave and have a go at a man or a mule."

"I saw their tracks up the mountain," Levi said. "They were trailin' the miners. There were tracks all over the place. I've been around wolves, but I've never come across a pack that big."

"The wolves up here are larger than most, and four or five will take down a man," Dennis said in a hushed voice. "A pack this big may take out two or three miners in one go. With that many hungry wolves together, there ain't nowhere safe."

"I guess we're gonna have to spend a week or two here in the compound until we see what happens," Rusty said. "To both the miners and the wolves. We still have plenty of traps that need repaired. We don't have to sit on our laurels all day, but I hope they go somewhere else or head back down the mountain, or they'll interfere with our trappin' season."

"And what about them?" Levi asked as he nodded toward the miners. They looked scared. They had good reason to be if Rusty got any angrier.

Rusty flashed his eyes from Levi to the miners. They seemed to shoot fiery daggers at the three as they stood quaking in their boots.

"Well, what are ya waitin' for?" Rusty asked. "I only wanted to ask ya a couple of questions. Go on now and git!"

"I thought we might spend the night here in your cabin or on the porch," the smallest miner said. His voice sounded less confident than he wished.

"Well, you thought wrong," Rusty spat. "Do you see a hotel or restaurant sign anywhere around here?"

"What?" the miner asked.

"What is not an answer!" Rusty yelled. "Where do y'all come from?"

"What?" the miner repeated, flustered and confused.

"What ain't no place I ever heard of," Rusty spat.

"What—I don't understand, mister," the miner said, panicked. He looked down at his boots and rubbed a hole in the dirt with the toe of his boot.

"Go get the shotgun, Angus," Rusty growled. "The one loaded with rock salt. We'll see if ya wanna move with your backside on fire."

The miners suddenly changed their minds about wanting to stay in the same house with Rusty Steel, and they grabbed their mules and headed up the trail with all the rest. The leader tugged on his mule to get him to move faster. He had heard about the men who lived all year in these mountains, and most of it was bad. He had been told the bunch from the compound was as ornery as they come.

"I swear," Angus spat. "If it ain't one thing, it's another. We've been on a streak of bad luck for some months now. Iffin I recollect right, it was ever since we ran into Levi and Forrester."

"Don't act a fool," Rusty spat, still angry. "Them boys ain't why we had bad luck. I figure we had good luck. We were attacked by the Comanche and lived and have survived every other thing that has happened since then. Yeah, I reckon the youngins be good luck."

Angus looked puzzled at Rusty and said, "I never looked at it that way." Then he smiled. "I reckon you're right. We're all still alive."

Of the trappers living in the compound, only one was superstitious to an extreme level. Of course, that was Angus. Dennis figured it was due to spending so much time with the Indians. They said their dances weren't like White or Black folks' dances. These were to speak to the gods and send a message or ask their gods for a favor, much like a rain dance or a war dance. They represented an action or need and weren't only for fun. Many had defined movements to their dance, unlike Angus, who cut it up something fierce but to his own tune and beat.

"How many of those miners you reckon there be, Levi?" Rusty Steel asked.

"I've seen fifteen so far, and I haven't actually been searching for them but a few hours," Forrester said. "Isn't that right, Levi?"

"Yup. If we've seen fifteen in one morning, who knows, there may be over a hundred by now," Levi said. "There's no way to know, really. I doubt the stories from the Indians will be long in comin', though."

The eight men gathered on Rusty's porch, sipping on piping hot java and puffing on ceramic or corncob pipes and cheroots. Rusty pulled a quid from his mouth and replaced it with a fresh twist of tobacco. He spat a yard of brown juice off the side of the porch.

"Well, this is a problem we never had before," Dennis said. "It's all a load of lies too. These men don't know what they're getting themselves into. I hope none of 'em brought any womenfolk with 'em. It'd be a shame for some wife to perish because of her crazy husband."

"What can we do about it?" Angus asked. "I don't dare head for my wife's tribe now. They might not be feeling too friendly to White folks."

"If we already know they're there, the Indians have

known for a day or so," Portland Pete said. "There ain't nothin' happens up here they don't know about before us."

"I felt bad you turned those men away that way," Levi said. "It wasn't very hospitable of ya."

"How many of those characters did you say you've seen, young man?" Rusty growled. "If it's even only fifteen of 'em, how are we gonna accommodate 'em? I ain't an unkind man, but there are limits. If you make the mistake of takin' in three, you'll end up with ten times that in a few days, iffin this is true about the newspaper article. We're gonna have to stay put and keep watch over things. Some of 'em will be thieves."

"Why do you think so bad of folks?" Levi asked.

"Because I'm twice your age and have seen enough of the human race to know how they be." Rusty smiled. "You can't be so affable all the time when living in a place frequented with dangerous people, son. You just watch, and you see how much of a ruckus this is gonna create. I wonder who in Sam Hill had it printed in the first place."

"Again, I say the Army is guilty of just this very such thing," Forrester said. "Bring in the foreigners and push out the Indians. That's their theory."

"From now on, we'll start locking the chicken house at night," Rusty said. "Now that we've got chickens and fresh eggs every day, I'd be mighty put out if somebody came around and stole 'em in the dark. The same goes for the horses and mules. During the day, they can stay in the corral and the chickens in the yard to hunt for worms. We'll all be here waitin' on the porch for the next bunch of fools. When folks got gold fever—where you find one, you find a dozen."

"Here come two more now." Forrester chuckled.

"And what is it you find so danged funny?" Rusty spat as he glared at the young ex-officer.

Forrester wasn't in the Army anymore. Unless you considered Rusty's bunch a sort of army. Their houses were built like little forts to fight the hostiles when they occasionally turned violent, like they had lately. They'd hardly had a week of peace and quiet since returning from the Rendezvous.

"I just find it odd that anybody can even find the cabins up here," Will replied. "They ain't even on the main trail up the mountain. If we're seeing people way over here, how many do you think might be traveling the main trail? I'm just saying that we have no idea of how many more miners are out there just about to pop up and give you an unwanted visit." Will Forrester gave Rusty a hint of a smile. He was angry, and Will didn't want to be considered among those in his poor favor.

NIGHT CREATURES

HE FROZE ON THE SPOT AS HIS EYES SHIFTED ACROSS THE night. He could see clearly despite the dark. He sniffed the air and, in a burst of energy, rushed through the forest as his heart redlined. He raced through the woods at neck-breaking speeds, letting his instincts lead him. His heart beat like a hammer in his chest. Feet pounded the ground behind him, but he was faster than them all. He felt no fear and was in control of his environment, punishing those who faltered. He caught an odor in the air and again, abruptly stopped.

The hairy beast sniffed the footprints as another twenty wolves followed the pack's alpha male. The occasional violent confrontation erupted among the canines. Teeth, fur, and claws tumbled for seconds until one of the dueling parties surrendered. They sought peace by touching each other's noses. The hierarchy is decided by the fittest, and all the pack follows their leader. They were all hungry, and the hungrier they got, the meaner they grew. The wolves' ribs showed how skinny they were during a time in the season when they should have had plenty to eat.

Its green eyes flashed around in the darkness. It turned and ran for the closest camp of miners. Until now, they'd made do with scraps left around the abandoned campfires—that and the occasional animal they managed to catch unawares. Lately, those were few and far between. The men they followed were not the best killers on the mountain. The most dangerous were the dark furry beasts that chased behind their leader and toward their next meal.

Dark gray fur surrounded the alpha male's eyes, and its long tongue hung out one side. It stopped and raised its snout to sniff the air. Its muscles tensed, and it burst out, leading the pack as they raced through the night again. Eighty feet pattered behind the lead wolf.

As the pack grew in numbers, they became braver and more brazen. Due to the lack of food, hunger was eating away at their stomachs. The mule stood outside the circle of light cast by the two miners' fire. They hadn't heard any signs of danger, but they were listening for Indians or grizzly bears.

Its heart redlined as it burst forward faster and faster, racing through the forest, dodging trees, jumping creeks, and leaping across springs. Its long canine teeth showed a dull yellow in the moonlight. It happened so suddenly the miner on guard duty fell off the stump he sat on but scrambled, terrified, to his feet. The head of the pack shot a glance at the two men sitting frozen with fear. For an instant, their eyes locked. Then it turned its head and latched onto the mule's throat like a steel trap.

Warm blood flowed into its mouth, just making it hungrier. The sound of twenty wolves growling and fighting over the same meal mesmerized the hunters. Their eyes spread wide in shock as the blood drained from their faces. For an instant, they seemed frozen on the spot from fright.

The guard and his partner hastily grabbed their weapons. One man shot a round off into the sky, but contrary to normal reactions, the maddened pack just tore at the flesh, more ravished than ever. The gunfire seemed to give them a sense of urgency. They no longer feared humans. There were so many of them that if they took a mind and gathered the confidence, they could have them both for supper. The acrid smell of blood filled the air, along with vicious snarls and the tearing of meat. The mule died silently with death's jaws clamping down on its windpipe.

One miner raised his long rifle, took a bead, and dropped it with one shot, and half the pack turned and looked their way. Their eyes narrowed as their senses filled with the odor of the aggressors—human beings, but they weren't afraid as they usually were. The smell of blood overwhelmed them, and they returned to their meal. Neither man was brave enough to mess with the wolves nor take another shot.

They didn't want to remind the ravenous beasts they were there. Even with extra pistols, they couldn't kill all the pack if they did attack. If they had gone without food for two weeks, they would be rabid. The miners located a tree and scurried up as fast as they could. They sat on a high limb, terrified, watching the pack devour the mule in minutes.

Wolves have over 200 million scent smells and can hear up to six miles in a forest. Their jaws have the crushing power of 1,500 pounds per square inch, allowing them to crunch ribs with their trap-like teeth like pieces of bacon. A wolf could eat up to twenty pounds of meat in one meal. They weren't known to kill a member of their pack, but if one died, they ate the dead body. Sometimes they did attack other packs, and then to the victors went the spoils.

The miners cowered high in a tree behind branches, hoping the wild wolves would forget about them with fresh meal from the mule at their feet. They went through the meat on the mule like a scythe through hay.

The alpha male was woolly and nearly black. Its green eyes appeared dead. The hair on his back stood on end, and his tail pointed up, showing his aggression. His pointed ears shifted to capture the slightest sounds. The wolf didn't think so much as sense what its next move would be. His instinctive reflex actions drove him as he sought to take the next victim down. They needed four hundred pounds of meat a day to feed twenty wolves. His job was far from finished.

The miners must have had angels watching over them because another smell changed the wolf pack's direction, and off they shot after some new prey. The men in the tree were in shock. They didn't come down until the following morning. They had never seen anything like the wolf attack and hoped they never did again.

"I think we made a mistake, coming up here," Lester said.

"I agree with ya," Robert replied. "And here I was worried about grizzly bears and Indians. I reckon we've done bit off more than we can chew, Lester. I say we turn around and go back the way we came."

Every time the moonlight flashed in the alpha

male's eyes, they turned from green to blood red. At a dead run, it sniffed the hundreds of odors in its environment as it picked out its prey. It roared through the forest with the rest of the pack on its heels. Its massive paws dug its claws in as it raced into a turn, and the prey just came into sight.

The massive canine lunged at the man snoring under the blanket. The first thing the human knew was when the large wolf sank its long teeth into his neck. He flailed his arms, but the rest of the pack caught up, and dozens of fangs sank into every part of his body. He was still conscious when they ripped his guts open and began to feed on their preferred part of fresh prey—the stomach and intestines. The leader of the pack stood back and let the weaker wolves have their feed. Blood dripped from the matted hair on its chin.

Bones cracked, and their marrow was eaten. When the pack of wild wolves was done, little was left for the vultures. Only the man's hair and skull lay on the ground on a soft bed of leaves. His face had been eaten away, but the wolves' mouths weren't large enough to get around his big head to crack it open, so the skull was intact. A single vulture circled above and finally folded its wings and dropped into a glide and landed on the miner's remains. It picked at the lice in what was left of his hair.

All night the alpha male tore through the darkness with twenty wolves on its heels. They devoured every animal in their path. Finally exhausted and full, they found a place in the soft grass to lie. They curled up, all pressed together, sharing their warmth, and slept. Some quivered, and their feet moved as they dreamed. Only the leader slept apart, with one eye open. He protected the rest of the pack from the dangerous elements and their natural enemies.

Grizzlies killed and ate wolves. When they were hungry enough, they ate the odd human too. The only other enemy worthy of their fame were human beings. The Indian Nations left the wolves alone for the most part, as they formed part of many of their traditions. Some even believed their tribes came from wolves, like the Tonkawa. Alone, they were careful and not much of a threat, but when in large, hungry packs of wolves, they were more dangerous than the fiercest grizzly bear.

Despite their quiet, humble appearance while they were asleep, when they awakened, they would continue on their never-ending search for food. As they slept, they looked like friendly house pets. When they awoke, they would convert into the ravenous beasts they truly were. What or who would be their next meal? Now there was a pack of killer wolves on the mountain; every human being that traveled alone was at risk, and even a few that traveled in twos or threes. It appeared this pack had evolved to a point that it no longer had any fear of human beings.

TENT CITY

As the miners arrived at the base of the mountains near the tree line, they naturally gravitated toward each other. Cid Maelstrom and Rex Leonard were the first to arrive. They immediately erected a tent and stored their supplies. They intended to go out and look for a spot to mine the following morning. They would start in the rivers and streams and see if there were signs of gold in the sludge at the bottom. When they found traces of gold in their slush pans, they would have to determine from where it came. Once located, they would dig into the mountain, looking for a vein of gold.

They seemed to come in twos and threes for the most part. When they had all set out for the race to be the first to claim a strike, there were said to have been a couple of stragglers. One, they weren't even sure made it out of town because he was so drunk. There was always someone who traveled alone despite the warnings. As the day passed, more men and even a few wives showed up at the soon-to-be tent city for the miners. More than twenty long-haired, unshaven men built campfires and erected small tents. It looked like they were digging in and planned to stay. Nobody thought to ask for the local Indians' permission. They were unknowingly being spied on as they went about their day.

They made a rope corral for the livestock when not in use and used horses to check out the lay of the land and where gold would most likely form. A few of the men even knew what they were doing, but for the most part, they were fools chasing a dream. Or, in some cases, desperate people hoping for one last chance at luck. A few husbands were even running away from their responsibilities and their wives to start new lives in the wilderness of the Wild West, where it was easy to change your name.

They were people who had fallen on hard times and saw no recourse but to leave and start over. Maybe if they were lucky, some could return home and live happy lives. Then again, some would be unlucky, and they would remain where they lost their lives over such a foolish venture.

The smell of salted pork and beans floated through the air as a miner whistled a sparky tune. Somebody jumped in on a juice harp, and soon, the happy notes of a harmonica joined in. Some men lingered the whole day in the camp to rest and organize themselves, while others dropped their goods next to somebody's tent and rushed off to find a stake. Most of them had gold fever so bad they had lost all sense and reason. A few even had no direction or honor before embarking on their search for their fortunes.

Some of them might find their fortunes in one way or another, but the others would suffer all the mountains had to throw at them. A few would die, and others would survive to walk back down the mountain. As time passed and more directionless people showed up, Cid and Rex saw they had stumbled onto a folly and appeared to be the leaders.

Cid had selected the place where he and Rex would put their miners' tent because of two rocks that would serve as seats. They built a fire before the stones and had a view of the growing camp. Both men had mined the 1803 gold discovery in Cabarrus County, North Carolina, the first documented gold strike in the United States. They remembered the craziness from men with gold fever. It looked like it was about to happen again. All they were missing was the gold.

That had been more than thirty years ago, and now the two miners were pushing sixty years old. They had been two of the lucky ones back then. They had found enough gold to live a life of leisure—at least until now. It was a funny thing, money. It was hard as the dickens to acquire in large quantities but was even harder to keep for long. Most fortunes are spent or lost before a man's death.

These two were such men. They had lived well for many years, but that had come to an end. Now, they found themselves where they were three decades earlier: looking for another needle in a haystack to make them rich again. The lack of money after so many years wealthy didn't sit well with the pair.

When they caught wind of the advertisement in the newspaper, they jumped right into action. That old gold fever had bitten them again. Like the first time, they ran off, knowing little of where they were going. All they knew was that this time, they had to travel across the country. Without their friend from Boise who wrote informed them about the newspaper article, they would have picked a more suitable place.

They already questioned their supplies in the face of the winter. They thought there would be much more game than there was. They had only heard stories about the blizzards and the grizzly bears. Nobody seemed even to consider the Indians. Everybody was so excited about the possible gold strike they forgot all the dangers and threw caution to the wind.

Cid wondered what planet these people came from. Many of them sure didn't look like they came from any semblance of civilization. They looked like the scraggliest bunch of miners he had ever seen. A more unlikely crowd he would never expect, but there still might be more to come. The two mining partners had seen it all happen before. The culprit was usually some newspaper somewhere that said somebody had struck it rich, and miners came out of the woodwork like termites. Everybody believed they, too, would strike it rich this time. Once again, it was a case of everybody repeating the same mistakes over and over again, expecting different results.

Now, they sat and watched as more miners arrived. They began to wonder about the newspaper article. Of course, newspapers were known to exaggerate but usually not tell an out-and-out lie. Then, there was that minor detail that there was no mention of who it was who struck it rich and where he was other than the vast Rocky Mountain Range.

This dawned on them both as they sat and watched one fool crazier than the next arrive during a long and unfortunate day. Too many people were coming and way too fast. Fifty miners could be roaming the mountains in a day or two looking for that pot of gold at the end of the rainbow. Rex and Cid suddenly realized they were right in the middle of wild Indian territory, and they knew diddly squat about these people. Would they be friendly like the Cherokee, or would they be vicious, as the newspapers had portrayed the Comanche and their warriors? That all remained to be seen. The two experienced miners didn't even like the look of some of the so-called miners. They looked more like low-lives and thieves than honest men panning for gold.

In no time, it looked like a circus right there between the mountain men's compound and the big Crow camp. The Indians must already know they were there, but as Cid and Rex lived back East where Indians were peaceful, they hadn't added hostile Indians to the formula. Neither man had ever read the dime novels or newspaper articles about the wild and aggressive Indians of the West. They had only heard about the Comanche, and they were said to be far to the south.

Of course, they had heard stories, but they believed most of them were so outlandish that they considered them lies. Back East, nobody paid much attention to the Indians. Then again, there they were a minority, but out in the wilderness, they were the majority. Most miners brought a good supply of rot-gut whiskey or white lightning to keep them warm at night. So the liquor flowed as soon as they arrived at what they believed was their destination. Time would tell if it was or not.

"Whatcha think, Rex?" Cid asked.

"What do I think about what?" Rex replied. "You mean that carnival that's arriving behind us? I thought we were gonna all split up, not make a tent city in the middle of the wilderness. I wonder how many more miners are gonna show? It could go on like this for days. It depends on how many men get the fever, like us." He laughed even though his partner didn't. Cid didn't see anything funny about their situation.

"Oh, yeah, that too," Cid replied with furrowed brow as his eyes narrowed. "What I meant was, did we screw up coming here with so little information? I didn't think about it much on the way here because I was focused on the trip. Now that I see the kind of people that tagged along, I don't like it so much anymore."

"Don't you think it's too late to have second thoughts?" Rex asked. "These fools aren't miners. We've worked hand-in-hand with the real deal, but these people aren't anything like them. Heck, you even studied some geology. If there's gold out there, we have the best chance of finding it before any of these losers."

"I wouldn't be surprised if there were an onery one or two in the crowd, if not more," Cid said as he eyed the people making camps much like theirs. "You know it always ends up the same. If and when we find some gold or silver and move our tent, everybody else will claim as close to ours as possible, and the same tent city will be moved to the gold. If several prospectors strike it rich, usually a town replaces the tents with real wooden buildings and the works. We've seen it happen for years, but we didn't need the money back then. I reckon times change whether we like it or not."

"I never thought we'd live long enough to spend it all," Rex huffed. "Then again, most folks don't live past fifty out here. We're a couple of the lucky ones. I wonder if we're gonna be that fortunate three decades later."

"I don't know if livin' so long has been a blessing or a burden?" Cid said. "Now that we spent all the money and we're aging fast, we have to start out all over again. If I had died last year, it would have been better timing."

Cid sniffed the air like a dog. "I can smell the fever in the air. Everybody here's got it, or they wouldn't be here. Any sane man would know better, but here we are, just like them dumb sons of guns."

"You might as well stop complaining about it. We're already here, and nothing's going to change that," Rex said. "Look at it as an adventure. We haven't been on a real journey for years, amigo. We must be getting old, but we ain't so old that we didn't come. That ought to count for something, don't you think?"

As the night neared, the two old friends remained on their stones like little thrones overlooking the newly emerged city of poles and cloth. The sun disappeared behind the mountains like a rock, leaving everything outside the camp in total darkness. They hastily made fires near the horses and tied them to trees. There were horse thieves everywhere, even in places where it looked like there lived none.

Much to Cid and Rex's disappointment, the partying got louder as the night went on. The men who had arrived, dropped their belongings and ridden off to check things out, returned and joined the already over-populated party.

"At least these fools will be too drunk to get up early and set out to see if there's gold in these mountains," Cid said. "I doubt half of 'em get up before midday. I'm gonna try to get some shuteye despite the noise. I want to be at my best tomorrow; the last thing I want is a hangover with a bad headache. This just confirms they're all a bunch of fools."

"I agree," Rex said. "Let's get some sleep so we can

get up early and get out of here before the others are awake, so they can't follow us."

"They did a pretty good job of following us up here so far, so I doubt we'll shake them all. The tracks are too clear with the frost. Even a fool can track in this weather. Maybe we can find some shale and rock to make them lose our trail. What we don't want is twenty more miners digging all around us. You know how they were when they got the fever. Especially the ones that don't know what they're doing."

"Yeah," Rex said. "It's always the same. More than half never mined in their lives, so they look for somebody who knows what they're doing and tag along the best they can. Anybody who waits and hopes to strike it rich by another man's work is a lazy dog."

"I figure if we move fast, we can find a stream or rock trail to throw them off our scent," Cid said. "We're gonna have to make sure we lose them before we start looking for real. This is going to cost us half a day. What looked like something too good to be true just turned out confirmed. It is too good to be true."

"Well, now we're here, partner," Rex replied, "so we're gonna have to manage with what we have to work with."

"How many of these buffoons do ya think are outlaws who are only here to steal whatever we find?" Cid asked.

"We'll know who they are in a couple of days because they'll be the ones that hardly go out and search for gold. They'll be waiting behind to rob whoever strikes it rich first. After two or three days, they'll be easy enough to pick out."

The party in the newly erected tent city went on

nearly all night. Just like Rex and Cid predicted, half the camp didn't wake up until well past noon, so it was too late for them. Others had refrained from getting dead drunk the night before and got up with the sun. By then, both experienced miners, although aged, had long gone. They were trudging up the mountain like they were back at home. Sometimes they walked within mere feet of Crow Indians who were spying on everything they all did. Of course, such an invasion could never go unnoticed or unavenged.

This was a flagrant breach of trespassing, and many of them were there. Some were armed to the teeth like Cid and Rex, but others had a single one-shot pistol to defend themselves. These stayed as close to the group as they could.

When Cid and Rex snuck off into the dark of early morning, nobody saw them but Hachta and two of his warrior braves. They exchanged looks, confirming what they already suspected. These men were in the mountains looking for the yellow rocks that made White men crazy. Still, they didn't quite understand, as there had never been any gold found in the Rocky Mountains. Then again, many of the Rockies were still unexplored, at least by the White man.

Although they had successfully escaped the camp without waking a single miner, they still had a terrible feeling in their guts, like something wasn't right.

It may have been their primal instincts telling them that there was danger lurking out in front of them. They couldn't shake the feeling that they were being watched.

RUSTY'S PORCH

THE FOLLOWING DAY, LEVI, FORRESTER, ANGUS, AND
Rusty were sleeping in the cabin, despite the rooster
crowing out back, wanting out of the chicken house.
McFarlin snored like a mule and even blubbered his
lips with each exhale. Finally, Levi couldn't sleep any
longer, and he threw back his buffalo hide and swung
his feet onto a cold floor. He pulled on his beaded
moccasins and rekindled the fire. In five minutes, hot
java bubbled from the coffee pot spout. He worked in
the small kitchen at the back of the cabin as silently as
possible.

Forrester was awake but was staring at the ceiling.
He rubbed his eyes with the heel of his hands and
blinked. He stretched into a yawn and slipped on his
military-issue boots. His saber hung beside his bed, but
he didn't often wear it any longer. It must have brought
too many bad memories of losing a limb. The cabin was
built of roughhewn logs sealed with mud and straw. An
array of rifles hung on the walls, so they were handy if

needed. Four 54-caliber Hawken rifles hung above the fireplace.

They quietly made some frying pan biscuits. When they were done, they planned to take it outside to enjoy the early morning on the porch and not wake the others. After breakfast, they would set the horses and mules loose in the corral and let the chickens out onto the yard.

They fried up four eggs and slipped them between sliced biscuits. Steam rose as they smelled the aroma of freshly made breakfast. The yolk melted into butter and bun when they bit into the biscuits. They sipped at their coffee. Then they heard Rusty Steel grumble, so they grabbed their food and refreshments and headed for the porch.

They didn't notice anything different as they sat down and devoured the day's first meal. The friends silently sipped on piping hot coffee. That was when they saw the two strangers sleeping on the edge of their porch. Two more lay asleep beside the chicken coop across the yard. Levi's face instantly turned red. They would have to pay the price if they'd been at the chickens.

The planks groaned under the weight of the six-foot-seven giant. He kicked the first miner in the back-side. The blow landed harder than he intended. The sleeping miner abruptly awoke, blinking his eyes as he stared up at the large man.

"What are you doin' on our porch?" Levi growled. "Are those two over there with ya?"

"Hey, what's the big idea?" he said. Then he saw the size of the man who'd kicked him, and his mouth became a gash.

"Rusty!" Levi shouted. "You better come out here and see this!"

An apparently peaceful night of sleep for the strangers abruptly ended, and everything suddenly went down the pipes. These men had knowingly trespassed, hoping the inhabitants of the cabins had kind Christian souls and would give them shelter and maybe food. They weren't very good hunters and could hardly feed themselves. They were just more fools with gold fever.

Feet stomped on the floor as Rusty Steel stormed out the door with a shotgun in his hands. He opened the breech and casually sipped in two fresh shells.

"What's all the shouting about?" Rusty asked as he locked eyes with Johnson.

"Them two critters right there be the problem," Levi replied. "There be two more of them over by our chickens. There ain't nothing I hate more than an egg thief."

"Do you know how long I've waited to have eggs up here?" Rusty asked. He instantly became furious. "I didn't hear you ask permission to come and sleep on my porch or even enter our compound. Who do you morons think you are just walking up and makin' yourselves at home? It's a good thing we had the cabin battened down, and we didn't hear ya, or we'd have shot y'all for trespassing in the dark."

Rusty pulled the hammers back on the shotgun, one at a time, breaking the sudden silence. The clicking sound got everybody's attention. The miners visibly grew nervous.

"Which one of you two dummies wanna get shot first?" Rusty asked all matter of fact like. "Come on. Speak up. I ain't got all day."

The miners' eyes spread wide, and their mouths moved, but no words came out. They were suddenly looking down the dark barrels of a shotgun, and their stomachs turned to jelly.

"You wouldn't shoot 'im for sleepin' on the porch, would ya?" Levi asked, aghast. "Whatcha going to do, Rusty—I mean really? Iffin ya want, I'll run 'em off for ya. There's no need to get mean."

"Stay out of this, Mr. Johnson," Rusty said as serious as death. "Which one of ya is gonna get shot first? If I were you two, I'd have already begun runnin' as hard as I could. Now git, or I'll shoot ya where ya lay."

Both miners scrambled to their feet and ran for the edge of the porch and into the yard as they raced for the chicken house. Levi jumped in shock when to his surprise, he heard the blast from the shotgun ring in his ears. Right after the first came a second round. He never thought Rusty would go so far as to shoot the trespassers. He looked from Steel to the fleeing miners, expecting to see them dead in the middle of the yard. Instead, he saw two men running hard, jumping as they rubbed the rock salt stuck in their backsides.

The graying mountain man laughed as Forrester joined in. Levi didn't know what to think. Rusty seemed to surprise him at every turn. He always thought he was doing one thing when he was doing another.

Rusty gave them both a good dose of salt, which stung like the dickens when it broke the skin. The two yowled and cried all the way out of sight. They jumped up and down like they had sat on a nest of fire ants. They could still hear them after they disappeared, running through the woods.

The other two men near the chicken house looked

on in shock and a little wonder. One miner sat up, and a stolen egg rolled out of his pocket and across the ground. Rusty was already removing the empty hulls and reloading two fresh shells.

Both men grabbed their things and ran out of the yard and through the fence before they got a backside full of rock salt too. They scattered in the wind like chickens from a fox in a hen house.

"Maybe that'll send a message to that bunch we don't want 'em around here," Rusty grumbled. "You saw they were stealin' our eggs, didn't cha? That's more than I can tolerate."

"It looks like those gold fiends are gonna be givin' us trouble," Angus spat like it was a dirty word. He stood at the door in a pair of red long-johns. He scratched his unruly hair with one hand and his scraggly beard with the other. He chuckled at the sight of the two buckshot trespassers. "Them two are gonna remember you for a spell, and they won't be getting no sleep tonight either. Not unless they got a real good friend that's willin' to pull them bits of salt out one piece at a time out of their backsides. Heck, it won't kill 'em. In a few days, their bodies will absorb the salt, and they'll have a bunch of little scabs. They'll have to be careful not to let 'em get infected."

"One thing for sure, they won't be lazy and sittin' around on their laurels." Levi laughed. "I doubt they be sittin' at all."

They all got a good laugh when Rusty dealt with the trespassers. The problem was he knew this wouldn't be the last of strangers. This was the second day, and they still had miners climbing up the mountain. Seven had passed by their compound already. They didn't doubt for a moment there were others taking different trails up. The cabins were off a side trail and not on the primary way to the top. When they came to live on the mountain, it was to get away from people like these. Men who were greedy for something free. Everybody was looking for a handout instead of working for their money.

"I figure out of the whole bunch there won't be but two, three, maybe four miners that are for real," Rusty said. "The rest probably believe they'll pick up gold nuggets right off the ground and call themselves rich. It's a labor-intensive job and ain't for the lazy. It takes weeks of hard work with long days, mostly digging up nothing of value. It's like fishing in a pond when you don't know if there are any fish in it or not. It's a fool's game, but somebody occasionally wins a prize if they don't perish first."

"So, what in the world are we gonna do with these trespassers?" Angus asked. "I can't see lettin' anymore into the compound. If they latch on to something that isn't theirs, we'll have to take it personally. I'd rather not shoot anybody this week. We've seen enough violence and had enough problems of late."

Sam, Pete, Bob, and Dennis were up and heading for Steel's porch. Soon all eight of the men were grumbling over the situation. They had just gotten rid of a few buffalo hunters, and they thought that was bad. Now they were facing who knew how many miners who had descended on their mountain claiming there was gold there when everybody knew there wasn't.

"What are we gonna do about these trespassers?" Syracuse Sam asked. "The miners are droppin' in on us like flies. There must be some way we can scare 'em off, but it has to be good, so they don't come back."

He removed his hat, exposing his scar where he had been scalped. He was one of the few men who had it happen to survive the ordeal. It did leave him a bit paranoid of Indians and strangers, though. Some wicked and evil men had passed through these mountains at one time or another, and Angus was dead intent on avoiding any more run-ins with wicked men.

Everybody pulled up a chair as Levi and Forrester went to the chicken coop to collect the eggs and to let the fowl out. That and water and feed the horses before they set them free to run around the corral. As soon as the white stallion stomped out the door, his eyes flashed defiantly at everyone except his master. It was like he was daring anyone to try and mount him. Forrester and his horse seemed inseparable.

Every Indian in the mountain had eyeballed the stallion, but most of them saw straight away they wouldn't be able to dominate such an animal. This stallion would choose who his rider was and not the other way around. It was headstrong and as fast as the wind. The captain had had it since back at West Point and brought it with him when he came west to the frontier forts in Kansas. He had always dreamed of riding into battle with his stallion. He had done just that, and it turned out to be nothing like he had imagined. He wondered how many men had felt the same in the past. Knowing in their minds they were on the verge of victory, then their hearts sank when they were defeated and the battle didn't pan out like expected.

"Where ya figure all these folks have ridden off to, Rusty?" Levi asked. "All of 'em are headin' up the mountain when this time of year they should be heading down."

"There's a network of caves and crevices just below the tree line along the same trail," Rusty replied. "I reckon they've bivouacked there and will go out mining of a morning and back of an evening until somebody sees some good prospects. Then they'll all run like fools to wherever the other folks said they found gold. A man with gold fever is the biggest sucker in the world, and there's nothing like 'im. It's an ailment that wipes out all reason in a man's mind, and the only thing he can think about is the yellow gold he's gonna dig out of the mountain. They all be sure they'll strike it rich unless there're some pros in the group. Only they will know the hard brutal truth of the matter is, there ain't nothing easy about mining for gold."

They spent the day on the porch looking out for trespassers and chicken thieves. If you weren't careful, a man could even lose a mule or a horse to the outlaws that came up to rob the ones who strike it rich. But the men on the porch had no doubt there was no gold on their mountain, so they expected the bunch to head back down shortly but not as fast as they had climbed up. Then they would return defeated and would have realized they had gone on no more than a folly. Some of them would meekly descend the mountain and accept the hand they were dealt; others would take it badly and look for something to steal to make their trip worthwhile.

"I reckon we best get all the pelts into the cabin," Levi said. "We've already lost half a day's eggs and a chicken."

"You mean to tell me them fools that were sleeping

on our property stole our eggs and a chicken?" Rusty spat. "Next time, I'm gonna use lead pellets instead of rock salt on those rascals."

"Come on, Forrester," Levi said. "Let's get the valuables out of the barn and stables before we lose everything we've got. That lot will be bad enough coming up, but when they head back down without their gold, they ain't gonna be happy. I reckon they may have a go at anything that's not tied down."

"In the Army, we shoot thieves," Forrester said.

"From now on, in our compound, we shoot thieves too," Rusty growled. "Even if it's just a chicken. The intent is just the same. They'll be takin' food out of our mouths. That's a serious offense in the wilderness. It could cost a man's life."

"I wish Green Leaves was here," Angus said. "I worry about so many White strangers up on the mountain. It's gonna get the Crow all riled up, and there's no tellin' what they'll do."

"Get some guns out here on the porch, boys." Rusty smiled. "The next strangers that show up here, we're gonna have a turkey shoot."

CID & REX

As they traveled through the darkness, frosted grass crunched under their feet. The horses blew, and the mules hee-hawed as they climbed up a steeper grade. The going was getting rougher by the mile. In the near distance, they could see where the tree line ended. Beyond that, hope for food was limited to the occasional mountain goat. All the while, Rex kept looking for geological signs of the proper rock formations where gold could be located. So far, he hadn't seen anything of interest. Cid kept an eye out for food, but he didn't see anything in time to get a shot off. The few animals he saw were skittish.

When they arrived at a disturbed rock formation and several caves, they decided this was where they were going to make their first test and see if there were any traces of gold. Besides the large stones and cliffs was a spring where water ran through a maze of rocks and crevices to unload in an arch into a deep pond. A steady bubbling of water was heard in the background. It was so crystalline you could see fish dart across the bottom of the sand. The overflow of that continued down the mountain via two more runoff creeks.

"We've got plenty of water here and some natural caves," Rex said. "That'll save us a heap of digging to see if there are any traces of gold or not. I wonder if anybody has ever been here—you know, folks like us. It looks like unseen land to me."

"Unseen land with a trail?" Cid asked as his brow furrowed. "And how do you figure that works?"

"Just because there's a trail doesn't mean humans made it. I heard these forests are teeming with wild game, and some are plenty big enough to make that narrow path."

"Well, everything we've heard up till now has all been lies because there ain't no game," Cid said. "It's probably a lie that there's gold up here too."

They unloaded the mules of the few tools they brought along with a torch, which was for just such an occasion. They had only hoped they would find a cave or two to see what the layers of the earth were made of. They hit the jackpot: that and broken cliffs from earth movements to see how the earth had changed geologically over the past centuries.

The old miners hobbled their horses and mules and climbed the steep path to the caves' entrances. There were three visible from where they stood. They believed there might be more, farther along. When they got to the top, they saw the fourth. It was the largest of all, with an opening twice the height of a man.

"I wonder if grizzly bears live in these caves," Rex said. "Everybody's heard of Rocky Mountain grizzlies."

"Why did you have to go and put such ideas in my head right now?" Cid retorted. "Now I'll feel nervous the whole time we're inside checking for gold. Dagnabbit, grizzly bears. Can't you ever think positive?"

"I wouldn't have mentioned it unless I thought it was a real possibility," Rex said. "Just thinking about it gives me the jitters, too, but it's better if we're prepared in case one does live in there."

Cid shot a dirty look over his shoulder and continued leading the way. The higher they went, the narrower the path got. By the time they reached the top, both men were so out of breath they were huffing like Baldwin locomotives. They didn't notice the smell of rotten meat or the sun-bleached bones at the edge of the large entrance. They were afraid of bears, but they never thought to look for signs of their presence. After their mining experience back East, they thought they were pros, but things were different in the wilderness of the Rocky Mountains.

Back East wasn't as difficult as the climb up the Rockies, not to mention all the other dangers in the mountains other than what the miners saw right before their eyes. They were blissfully oblivious they were being watched the whole time. Maybe even by more men and animals than one or two. There was nothing worse than men in situations far out of their leagues who thought they knew what they were doing.

Rex lit the torch, and Cid wrapped a pair of wire-rimmed glasses over his cauliflower ears. He scratched his short nose and wiped his pouty lips with the back of his hand. Gray hair grew over his head and face and out of his nose and ears. He had a perpetual tobacco quid in his cheek; try as he may, he was a lousy shot when he spat.

"Come on," Rex said as he held the torch in one

hand and a single-shot pistol in the other. The gun trembled in his hand. His thumb was on the hammer, and he followed the barrel and the torch's light into the darkness. It was so dense they could only see eight feet before them. The flame cast dancing shadows on the cave's walls. "If we don't go now, I may not be brave enough to go later."

They shared an uncomfortable silence. Neither miner dared speak for fear that some wild beast living deep in the mountain would awaken and have them for lunch—that and the fear of their voices cracking or not sounding as confident as they should. They inched deeper into the cave. Every twenty yards or so, they would stop, and Cid used the pick to cut into the rock. The echo of the digging rang through the cavern, but there was nothing they could do. They expected a monster grizzly bear to burst out of the dark at any minute, but nothing appeared.

They had been in the cave for nearly an hour. It was hot deep in the side of the mountain. The cave gradually shrank in size until the ceiling was just overhead. Then they walked into a large room made of natural rock. Cid and Rex dove for the floor when the cloud of black creatures broke free from their clutches to the ceiling. They flew like one black cloud along the cave and out the entrance. Both men had their faces buried in the dirt. When they raised their heads, the torch was half-extinguished. In the little light, they could only see their brown faces and the whites of their eyes.

Now their hearts hammered between their temples. Glistening sweat was visible on their faces by the torchlight. Neither man dared breathe as they went even farther into the beast's guts. They were both ready to turn and run at the slightest sound or motion. The bats had shattered their nerves, and now they went forward for no more reason than not to return to the creatures of the night. They had heard stories of how they sucked the blood from humans, and they didn't want to have anything to do with that. Hopefully, there would be another entrance at the end of the tunnel, and they could come out another way.

"Why do I feel like we're walking into the jaws of a monster?" Rex whispered.

"Hush up," Cid spat. "I'm trying to listen. Did you hear that? Hush now. There it is again."

Somewhere deep in the bowels of the cave came a rumbling sound. Cid pulled his pistol as he swung the pick over his shoulder, and they inched forward. Deep in the mountain, there was the humming sound of Mother Earth. They wondered if it was inherent to the cave or mountain. They detected every tiny sound, no matter how small, now that paranoia was perched on their shoulders. They continued to venture deeper into the black cave, even though they thought they heard some living thing. They had no idea if it was man or beast.

Far down at what looked like the end of the tunnel, they finally saw the first sign of daylight. A ray of light shone through the shaft at the other end. They felt a bit more confident for the first time since they entered the cave. They even began to chuckle at their own fear. It still made them both nervous, though, despite their small relief.

Rex continued to lead the way as the mouth of the cave at the other end grew. Their visibility got better, but dark shadows loomed large down the sides of the cavern. Every step they made sounded like a fighting bull as it pounded the earth with its front hooves. It was amplified, making them all the more nervous.

Finally, Rex found the exit on the other side of the mountain. He walked out into the light and breathed a deep sigh of relief. He threw the torch into the dirt. He was hyperventilating and had to rest the heels of his hands on his knees as he recuperated. He had enough of the cave for one day.

"Man, oh, man, am I ever happy to be out of there," Rex said as he turned around, but to his surprise, Cid wasn't there. He looked back confused—then scared. He had just heard him behind him. He couldn't be far.

Rex peered into the entrance and whispered, "Cid, are you in there, pard? Don't play games. This ain't funny anymore."

Nobody answered, so he finally gathered enough courage to shout. "Cid! Come out of there right now. Are you injured, buddy?"

Rex didn't sound as confident as he had a moment before. If Cid didn't answer, it meant something had snatched him up, but how did it do it so quietly? If it was a bear, wouldn't Cid have had time to yell out? He figured it had to be something else. Maybe his partner banged his head on a low hanging rock and knocked himself out. Then he would be in need.

Now, Rex didn't know what to do. Of course, he knew what he should do, especially as Cid had been a close friend most of his life. Then again, there was whatever grabbed Cid so silently Rex didn't hear a thing. His stomach climbed to his mouth, and he turned to the side and retched. Sweat covered his face and dripped off his chin. He was on the verge of hysteria.

Get yourself under control, man, his mind screamed.

He carefully inched his way into the cave entrance and stretched his arm out with the torch. The fire made a circle at the opening, but he saw no sign of Cid or anything.

At this point, he believed there was only one thing to do. That was to return to the tent city and get some help to return and enter the cave again. But this time, with enough firepower to stop a grizzly or even two if that was what got Cid.

The situation overwhelmed Rex so much that he plopped down on the ground and wept. He didn't know if he was crying for his old friend or if he was weeping because of his own predicament—maybe both. He was lost as to what to do next and afraid to leave the cave if Cid came out and he wasn't there. Then again, he was worried for himself in case whatever got his friend was waiting to eat him too. Images of massively large beasts with three-inch teeth and claws filled his mind. He tried to push it aside and into a dark box, but he couldn't break the spell. He stood frozen on the spot, not knowing whether to go forward or backward. A vulture landed on a nearby tree, waiting for its dinner.

As he stood there, his friendship seemed to flash before his eyes. He remembered all the good things Cid had done for him over the years. Right then, he knew he had to go back in and find out what had happened to his best friend. He steeled himself to the task and took two steps into the cave. Suddenly, something snatched the torch out of his hand. It felt like the slap of a paw. The next blow came so swift and brutal that he never knew it was coming or felt its effect.

It hit him so hard that his neck snapped like a twig,

killing him instantly. The bear lumbered over to the still body. The beast looked puzzled as it nudged it with its snout. The bear was over seven feet tall and looked like a big male. It was upward of seven hundred pounds of muscle and fat standing over the dead body of Rex. Returning to find the body of his best friend didn't work out so well.

In the corner of the cavern sat Cid. He was cowering from the beast. Blood ran out of both his ears. He was completely deaf and couldn't hear a sound. He couldn't even remember exactly what had happened. When he looked up, he locked eyes with the bears, and it roared with such force Cid's hair fluttered, and spittle covered his face.

Immediately after, his lights went out, and he joined his best friend on the other side. The fear suddenly passed just as quickly as it had appeared, and he was at peace with himself and the world. As he passed, he didn't even remember the bear.

HACHTA

HACHTA CRAWLED CLOSER TO SHOW HOW BRAVE HE WAS. After the first day, the tent city appeared; they waited and watched along with a few of his warriors. On the second day, they began to make it a game. Sometimes, the campers came within six feet of where they hid when they went out to tend to their personal needs. The men who stayed back in the camp were drinking whiskey and didn't seem interested in chasing after the yellow mineral the White men liked so much.

Still, there were too many to attack at once. The war chief knew he would win, but he also knew he would lose more braves than was acceptable to his code of behavior. If they saw one, two, or three outside the compound, they would capture them and take them back to camp for the old maids to torture. They were the best. They were soured with their lives and took pride in inflicting pain on their enemies. It also appeased the women for a time so they wouldn't be so strappy with the tribal elders.

He counted seven men out of over thirty that arrived. A dozen tents were constructed, and it looked like they planned to stay. The others left in the morning, headed to the tree line, and returned in the afternoon. He knew what they were looking for, and they also knew there was none. They were fools following some gossip or an out-and-out lie.

Usually, the miners went outside their tent camp to tend to their needs accompanied by another. Sometimes, those who were drunk forgot they were in dangerous country and wandered out of the camp alone and into the woods, so no one smelled it.

The Irish miner staggered from the end of the camp and into the woods. He stopped and stared ahead wide-eyed. He walked a few more yards into the bush but he saw nothing. He saw a tree with big leaves, so he pulled off a half dozen and dropped his pants. With his britches to his ankles, two of Hachta's braves rushed the man from behind, and each grabbed an arm and carted off the small redhead so fast he had no time to defend himself—especially since he was drunk. He opened his mouth to scream, but nothing came out as his eyes popped out of their sockets, and his chin hit his chest. Fear had him in its grasp, and he was too scared to get a croak out of his mouth.

He was whisked away so quickly that it wasn't until that night that they discovered he was missing. Nobody had a clue of where he'd gone. The only thing they all remembered was that he was very drunk. He had vanished, and nobody even remembered his name. He was one of the few that had made the long trek alone and alive, only to disappear into the wilderness. They had no idea if he was killed by a wild animal or by hostile Indians.

Even though one of them had probably been killed, since he was nobody's friend, they didn't seem alarmed. The ones hunting for gold continued to leave in the morning and return in the afternoon. While they were gone now, one less remained in the camp.

Hachta chuckled to himself as he continued to spy on the trespassers. He was amazed when there was no reaction to them capturing one of the members of the miner's tribe. If it was that easy, why not take a couple more? It would make the members of the tribe happy. It would give them somebody to blame their empty bellies on.

That afternoon, they watched as the miners returned to their camp. On the first day, they were enthusiastic about hunting for gold. Now, on the third day, they were already grumbling. Living in the Rocky Mountains was proving to be more challenging than they had counted on, and things had yet to begin.

Hachta whispered with his warriors as they planned some fun. The bushes rustled behind them as two braves came in, running fast, bringing a bundle in their fists. They passed it to their war chief, and he shot off like a bullet for the center of the camp. The braves vanished instantly because they knew what was chasing them. As the Crow Indian war chief raced across the camp, a look of shock covered the miners' faces. Hachta tossed the bundle into one of the tents and continued to run for the other side of the camp. He caught them all by such surprise, nobody thought to take a shot at the crazy Indian.

Behind him came a raving mad mother bear. She roared and slashed her claws in the air. She sniffed for the scent of her baby and charged the camp. She knew exactly where her cub was. It was in the tent When she got to it, she ripped it to shreds. Her cub popped its head out of the sack, oblivious to the danger. It began to take little baby swipes at the sack as it played.

The mother wasn't in the playing mood as she tore into every human she could reach. It wasn't until her little cub disappeared into the woods that she turned and lumbered away, still groaning in protest. Hachta sat and laughed as he watched from high in a tree.

The following morning, Hachata took a dozen braves and followed some of the miners to see where they went. Maybe they would have another opportunity. Patience usually provided them some little window of convenience. That would be when they would strike, so they would have no loss of life.

He wondered what his friend, Rusty Steel, had to think about all these crazy people coming to the mountain at the end of summer. They all came there to look for something that wasn't theirs. As a war chief, he knew he couldn't let these people go about their way and do whatever they wanted. If he let them continue, more would come after them. Then his tribe would turn against him for not acting when he had the opportunity. He began to make plans to put an end to this and to ensure it never happened again.

This was going to be tricky too. He was aware that if they killed too many White men, the Army would come looking for them for revenge the following summer. He had to think of something that would send a message but not go so far as to start a small war. He would have to ponder it some more after they followed more miners. He had the hint of an idea, but it wouldn't be quite enough.

A few hours later, a dozen Crow warrior braves surrounded three miners. There were two men and a woman. The men used their picks to chip away at rocks as the woman filled buckets of ruin and carried them away. Twenty feet from the dig was a pile of rock and stones higher than a man's head and five times as wide.

Sweat glistened on the shirtless men. The woman stopped to pull her hair back and tie it with her bandana. She used her sleeve to wipe her brow. She sang *Three Acres and a Cow*, as the men hammered their picks.

They had come to America from an English working family to seek their fortune. Now, they were hunting for gold.

Hachta heard the woman sing:

You working men of England, one moment now attend. While I unfold the treatment of the poor upon this land. For nowadays the factory lords have brought the labor low. And daily are contributing plans to prove our overthrow. So arouse you sons of freedom, the world seems upside down. They scorn the poor man as a thief in country and in town.

She, her husband, and his friend had come over on the same ship only five years earlier. They were working hard to make it in America, where they said if a man worked hard, he could become rich. Times back in England became too challenging to survive; they had sold everything they had and boarded a ship for New York. Now, after five years, they still struggled to find the land of milk and honey the British newspaper talked about. They had been halfway across the country, and they hadn't found it yet. Maybe it lay there under their feet in the form of gold nuggets.

Despite the hardships they had experienced in America, they still thought it was better than where they came from, where starvation and famine was the new order of the day.

CAPTAIN FORRESTER

THEY WAITED FOR THE NEXT BUNCH OF MINERS TO PASS the compound. They sat patiently as they sipped on coffee laced with a dash of whiskey. Angus was fidgety, so he spent the day making biscuits and cornbread with gravy. Rusty Steel was so angry he was beyond himself. If it weren't necessary for them to stay to protect their livestock and possessions, he would have already been after the trespassers and thrown them off the mountain one way or another. They had his dander up, and he was itching for a fight.

"Whatcha think Hachta is gonna do about all these miners?" Levi asked. "I doubt he takes kindly to their presence."

"You never know," Forrester said. "By now, the whole bunch of them could be dead and scattered to the wind. We may have to go up later and bury what's left."

"I hope he scalps every last one of 'em," Rusty growled.

"Why, that's mighty harsh, ain't it?" Levi replied. "I'd never wish such a thing on our fellow man."

"They should have known better than to believe some lie in a newspaper that says anything about gold," Rusty said. "Ninety percent of the gossip about the stuff is all lies and fabrication. If there was gold up here, don't you think we would be rich by now?"

"I've been here the longest, and I've never heard any gossip of gold up this way," Mountain Dennis said. "If there was any around, I'd have found it by now. I did some prospecting myself during my first years and didn't come up with a thing."

"I always fancied goin' prospecting for a spell sometime in my life," Levi said. "You've got to admit, iffin it was true, it would be a heck of a temptation. Of course, I would go to someplace where they already found gold, so I knew I had at least a little chance."

"You have about as much chance as some New York City business fella smelling your fart from here in the Rockies," Rusty spat. "I don't give a dad-gummed about the gold. I'm worried about the wild game with all these people huntin'. It was already slim pickings, but now it's just gonna get worse. If the Crow does kill all White folks up there, the whole danged Army is going to be headin' this way."

"He's right, you know," Forrester said. "If there is a massacre, they'll come up here and kill a bunch of Indians even if they weren't the ones who did it. But they'll be here just the same, although not until next summer. The Army isn't made of fools, and they'll know that sending a patrol up here this time of year would be risky because the weather could change without much, if any, notice."

"I hope it snows tonight," Rusty growled. "I hope we get the biggest blizzard of the year tomorrow. Then we'll see how many of those crazy folks stay up here sleeping rough outside."

"That won't change these peoples' minds," Angus said. "Once the gold fever's gotcha, there ain't no talkin' sense to such fools."

"What we need is for Will Forrester here to come up with a plan to scare the dickens out of these folks as soon as they show up," Levi Johnson said. "What can we do to make anybody that sees it stop and turn around and go back the way they came?"

"Do we have any thin wooden posts? Maybe some pine about the size of a woman's wrist?" Forrester asked. The ex-Army captain's mind jumped into gear, the wheels began to turn, and he churned out an idea that would probably make a few people faint.

Forrester brought his stallion from the stables. He was saddled, and he pranced and stomped the ground with his front hooves as his owner led him to Rusty's cabin. He was so high-spirited that the captain was the only man that could ride him, and even he had trouble controlling the horse, but this was the high-spirited animal the captain had dreamed of riding into battle. He did find his fight with the Comanche, but they, unfortunately, lost the glorious battle Forrester had imagined.

Now, the ex-captain found himself in the last place he had imagined. He was living a life so different he never believed it possible. He was changing from a West Point officer to a mountain man, even if he was still a wannabe. He could feel the officer in him resist the change, but it was already done and now there was no going back.

He walked the horse to the hitching rail, slapped the

reins around the post, and took a seat. A series of posts were stuck out of the ground all around the compound. He and Levi resumed their game of mumbly peg they had started a couple of hours earlier.

"Does anybody remember how a Comanche screams?" Forrester asked.

"I remember it was the most blood-curdling sound I've ever heard," Levi said.

"If you don't know, I don't know who would, after having not one but two battles with them scallywags," Rusty said. "Close your eyes and remember back on the last clash. I can assure you it'll come back to ya right quick. A Comanche war cry ain't somethin' that a man easily forgets. I still hear 'em in my dreams."

"That's five out of five," Levi said proudly. "You know nobody can beat me at mumbly peg."

"Why don't you two young men play something more interesting than throwin' a knife in the dirt?" Angus chuckled. "Apart from dulling your blade, it requires no brains at all. I prefer backgammon. That's an intelligent man's game. At least there's more of a challenge and less chance of ending up with your knife in your foot."

"So, you're an intelligent man now, are ya?" Rusty laughed. "I bet if you teach these boys how to play all proper like, they'll be beatin' you in no time."

"Last time you tried, you didn't do a very good job of beating me, if I recollect correctly," Angus said as he wobbled his head.

They all heard a bird call, but Angus tilted his head, put his hand flat over his eyes, and searched for something.

"Come on in, darlin'!" Angus called out as he

grinned like a possum. "It's Green Leaves. If she's left camp, she's come here to tell us somethin' important. She doesn't like going out on the trail when White men are around. An Indian woman alone in the forest is in great danger. There's been plenty nabbed by buffalo hunters and used and left to die, if they didn't kill her right off. There's some mighty wicked men who occasionally come to these mountains."

The short Crow Indian woman came running to the cabin. She shot a suspicious glance over her shoulder.

"What's all the hurry, girl?" Angus asked.

"Hachta sent me," Green Leaves said. "He said for you all to stay in the compound. I'll stay here too. I was scared to death to come here, but I had to obey an order from a war chief. I feel better here with you, Angus. Somebody has to take care of you."

"Whatcha mean, we gotta stay in the compound?" Rusty retorted. "I don't like folk's tellin' me what to do. Even if they do outnumber us twenty to one."

"It is for your own good," Green Leaves said. "There are many angry warriors roaming the forest, and they may mistake you for the miners. Hachta asked you to please do as he asked. He knew you would not like to be ordered, so he asked to do it for your friendship. He is only trying to protect you, his friends, and control the situation, so too many White men aren't killed by Crow Indians."

"We have to stay here anyway, Rusty," Levi said. "If we all go, who's gonna watch the rest of the livestock, the chickens, and our things in the cabin? You know, if we leave the place alone, these miners will break in and make themselves at home. They already tried to do it with us in the house and all."

"Here come some now," Dennis said.

"I don't see anything," Forrester said as he stared down the trail, then shifted his eyes to the top of the compound.

Once again, the captain looked on, puzzled. How could these two tell if people were coming before he could? He had years of training in combat at West Point, but none of his studies seemed valuable in the Rocky Mountains. None of the theoretical situations appeared, and everything else imaginable was being thrown at them. He realized that here it was all about improvision regarding combative tactics.

"I can smell 'em too," Levi said.

"There you go again with the smelling," Will grumbled. He sniffed the air and said, "All I smell is coffee and tobacco. How can ya smell anything over that?"

"If ya don't already know, I don't see exactly how to tell ya." Levi laughed. "I reckon it's a gift given to us chosen few."

Five minutes later, two more miners passed by the compound and stopped. These were going back down the mountain. They had obviously run out of supplies. Their mule's back was barren of everything but a pick, a shovel, and a sluice pan. Nobody said a word to them. Their faces said it all. They wanted a place to sleep and food and who knew what else. Whatever they could get off these rugged characters sitting on the porch like they owned the mountain.

"Don't ya think we should help these poor folks?" Levi asked. "Look at them faces, Rusty. How can ya say no?"

"NO—that's how," Rusty spat. "Go get 'im, Captain. It's time to set your plan into action." He looked back at

Levi. "You sure are a sucker for a sad face. In the wilderness, every man has to carry his own weight. If we helped every one of these strangers that have passed by, we'd be out of food halfway through the winter. Ya have to use some common sense too, Levi. We can't jeopardize our winter just because these fools didn't plan properly. Do you see any Indians coming around and askin' for handouts of food and shelter? This ain't a hotel or restaurant, son. We can't go giving away our food no more than we would consider giving away our beaver pelts."

Forrester slipped his stallion's reins from the hitching rail and swung astride his massive horse. He elegantly galloped to the far end of the yard and turned. The stallion reared, and his sword flashed in his left hand as he gripped the reins in his teeth. The white stallion took off like a raging bull. As Forrester passed the post, he lopped the end off each one while screaming like a Comanche warrior and riding at full gallop. The ends of posts flew into the air. The message of what would happen to the heads of the miners if they stopped there was received loud and clear.

The miners who'd stopped before the cabins turned and ran down the mountain for their lives. Suddenly, they weren't hungry anymore. The seven mountain men on the porch all roared with laughter until they got a stitch. Now they were making the best of a bad situation and creating some entertainment for themselves. If they were stuck in the cabins for a few days, at least they would get a laugh or two out of the deal.

Forrester raced his stallion toward the porch, showing off. He slid to a stop and jumped off the horse in a single motion. As his boots hit the dirt, dust clouds appeared at his feet. He'd proved his horsemanship and then some. All the men cheered and slapped him on the back for the idea and the fine display of using an officer's saber. It was quite the show. Will felt better all the time.

He had lost his arm and proven he was just as much a man as before the loss. Levi was happy to see him feel good too. He had witnessed his fall from military grace firsthand, and he knew how much it hurt even though he never showed it. It had to be hard to lose something so quickly that you had worked toward for so many years.

"At least them miners were goin' down the mountain rather than up," Bob said as he twisted the end of his handlebar mustache. "I don't reckon they'll be headin' back this way anytime too soon."

"That's a good thing in itself," Mountain Dennis said as he smiled, and the sun sparked on his gold teeth. "At least they've stopped comin', and some are already headin' back down. I reckon they can't find enough to eat like most of us up here on the mountain."

THE LAST HUNT

DESPITE THE COMMOTION THE MINERS CREATED, IT WAS time for Rusty, Dennis, and Levi to head out and make one last attempt to find some meat to salt and save for the coming long winter. They had just enough to get by at the moment, but with so many Indians going hungry, they figured they best do what they could to help both themselves and those who shared the mountain.

"I'm gonna take you two to a secret spot of mine that I discovered nearly fifteen years back," Dennis whispered like he didn't want anybody to hear. "It's hard to get to, and we'll have to walk the mules. The horses ain't surefooted enough to make the last stretch, and we don't dare leave 'em hobbled, or they may not be there when we get back."

"I've got no problem with walkin'," Levi said. "I'd always rather walk when I hunt. All ya need is a noisy horse blowing and whinnying while you're takin' a bead to mess up a shot."

"And why are you telling me about this just now after living here for a decade beside you as your neighbor?" Rusty grumbled. "You'd have thought you might tell something like that to a friend."

"I don't tell you everything I know," Dennis retorted. "Just because you think you're God's gift to man don't mean that everybody agrees with ya. So, stop your grumbling, and let's get the mules rigged up and grab your guns. It may be best if we all go with extra pistols just in case we come by a bunch of Crow warriors who don't know the miners left the mountain yet."

"How long are we gonna be gone, Dennis?" Levi asked. He was in charge of packing the mule with food and supplies as he was the low man on the totem pole.

"It'll take us three days to get there," Dennis said. "We may push the mules and make it in two and a half. It's just far enough away so nobody runs across it by accident, and the passage is difficult enough to put most hunters off—even most Indians. I ain't been there for a spell—maybe a couple of years or so now. It'll be hiding in the small valley if there's any game around at all."

"I hope you're right, or by spring, we'll be surviving on what we can trap and eat and beans with salted pork. I don't fancy spending a winter eating beans every day."

The following morning, the three rode out. The whole compound was drinking coffee on Rusty's porch to see their buddies off. Everybody knew this hunt was of paramount importance for their winter's food supply. Maybe if they found a good spot for game, they could send Green Leaves to inform the Crow tribe. Anything they could do to help the relationship with the Indians. They knew that if the Indians wanted, they could push them off the mountain just as easily as they did the hunters, especially with the help of the pack of wolves and a grizzly bear of two.

The miners had been a perfect example of what happened to men and a few women when they set off with their minds full of gold fever. The next time those that had survived tried something so foolish, they would think again. It was dangerous to run off half-cocked and ill-prepared when venturing into the Rockies. It wasn't a place for most men. Only a chosen few were built to survive such conditions.

They set off at a trot as Dennis ran, taking the lead. Rusty was in the middle, and Levi Johnson took up drag. Johnson would run off the trail every few hours, swing around, and make a large circle to see if anybody was following, but now there was no one there. He closed his eyes and took a deep breath to smell all the odors provided by Mother Nature. He didn't smell anything alarming, so he turned back toward the leaders and raced into a long stride to catch up.

When he got Dennis and Rusty in sight again, he dropped down to a walk as his face glistened with sweat. Levi said, "There's nobody followin' us. Of that much, I'm sure."

"Well, it's about time we're alone again," Rusty Steel said. "I hate it when strangers present themselves at our houses uninvited. I have Angus working on a sign right now. Just in case the next strangers that come by haven't heard, we don't want visitors. As slow as he is, he probably won't have it done for a month."

That night, they made a fire under the stars. Everybody was in a strangely solemn mood. Maybe they all felt the change quickly happening in the wilderness. Each year, more and more people arrived at what was once their paradise. Of course, they still lived a blessed life, but now they saw that in a few years, they might have to find another place to live yet deeper into the foothills of the Rocky Mountains. The conversation was held to a minimum.

Levi took the first shift at guard that night while Angus snored like a bull, and Dennis slept with his head under his saddle to block the sound. Rusty had long gotten used to McFarlin, but it took Forrester and Johnson weeks to be able to close out the sound and achieve a night of deep sleep. Still, the solemn feeling affected the three.

Not because there was something to mourn but because they had made it through the last couple of weeks with only a chicken and a few eggs stolen. Still, something ate at their minds the whole way to Dennis's secret spot. All of them feared that, even though Dennis said it never failed to provide some wild game, all they were going to see were empty valleys, streams, and springs this year.

Is everything drying up and going to pieces like Angus always says it will, or will things slowly return to normal? Levi thought as he peered into the night.

They had put the fire out to sleep so they wouldn't draw any attention, and then their visibility would be the same as any other human that decided to pop up, as they had lately.

As they rode through the next day, it was almost like they were trying to slow down. They felt the later they saw the hard facts of the situation, the better. Yet the second night came and went. They weren't even tired because they walked at a leisurely pace, but on the third day, they all had to focus. They were far enough away from the cabins that if something happened, they would have too far to go to take cover. The path to the secret spot was overgrown with weeds and dangerous.

Now, the trail was up and down steep and narrow trails just wide enough for a mule. There was no way a horse would be surefooted enough to come this way if someone had ever even found it. At the last bit, there didn't even appear to be a track, but Dennis knew the way from years of visits. Still, he hadn't been back this way for over two years, so he had no idea who had been there. Hopefully, it was still the same untouched beauty he had seen and felt two years earlier.

The path got steeper and more complex until it appeared unpassable. What had initially brought Dennis to such an isolated place was beyond his friends' imagination. He finally stopped and turned his head from the top of the hill and back to his friends.

"It's just over that next rise above us," Dennis whispered. They didn't know if he spoke softly because he didn't want the animals in the valley to hear or because he was afraid of breaking some magic charm. He held his breath as Dennis scrambled up the steepest path for the last hundred yards. His mule groaned in protest.

Dennis was the first to arrive at the top. They had to climb up one at a time in case a mule or man lost its footing and fell thirty feet down the trail. If it was unlucky, it would continue down a couple hundred yards more and to its death—man or beast. Dennis didn't say a word as he reached the summit and stared into the valley.

"What's the matter, pard?" Rusty asked as he stumbled up the dangerous path with his trusty mule following him. She had no problem at all with the steep grade. Dennis didn't seem to hear him speak. He didn't answer or even look back their way.

When Rusty reached the top, he stood silent beside his old friend and fellow mountain man. Over the last ten or fifteen years, they had seen many changes in the wilderness. It looked like things were just getting worse all the time. This summer had been the most challenging despite adding two new men to the compound. They hadn't caused any trouble that couldn't be avoided, but something seemed to have accelerated the changes since their arrival.

Finally, it was Levi's turn. Neither of the men standing at the top of the hill said a word, nor did they look back at Johnson. It was like they were mesmerized by what they saw in the hidden valley. It was like they had forgotten he was even there. A bad feeling hit his stomach like a swift kick to the gut when a man was already down. He couldn't help but believe his and Forrester's arrival had something to do with the bad run of luck. Levi wasn't very superstitious but just enough to believe their futures may well be cursed.

When he looked back on everything that had happened since he left home, it seemed like he got caught up in a whirlwind, and he was still spinning around and around, waiting for it to spit him out and see where he was going to land next. So far, most of their decisions were not made by them but were forced on them by some experience or fate, like them running into the mountain men from the compound.

That had been a stroke of luck for them, and they got invited to a place to stay and the possibility of becoming the men of their dreams—at least Levi's. Now, he felt maybe they had brought a curse to the compound. The men who lived there said they had never experienced such a convoluted summer in all their years. It all started in Kansas.

Johnson had to pull Dot up the steep grade. She was afraid of the two-hundred-foot drop-off to their right. To their left, the canyon wall rose another hundred meters above them. Mountains towered all around them. Some with traces of snow were visible above the tree line. The air was much cooler than down by the cabins, and the lack of oxygen made it harder to breathe.

He had to pull hard the last few feet because the mule didn't want to budge. After several minutes of coaxing, Levi got her to move forward again. He held a carrot in his hand and coaxed her to the top. The whole time Dennis and Rusty acted like he wasn't even with them as they stared at the supposed magic valley with expressionless faces. Johnson figured if the news were good, they would be jumping up and down, but since there was no reaction, he believed that old bad luck that seemed to ride on his shoulder lately couldn't be bucked off.

When Levi Beaver Johnson struggled the last three feet to the top and finally lifted his eyes from the trail, his heart stopped and skipped a few beats. He felt like he couldn't breathe. A bead of sweat cut a path in the dust down the side of his face. Dennis and Rusty didn't even realize he was there. Nothing but brown woolly fur covered the valley at their feet some thirty meters below them. It ran from their feet to some ten miles down the valley's length. It was one of the grandest wonders of Mother Nature left on earth. Levi forgot where he was and what he was there for.

After over an hour, Rusty cleared his throat, wiped a

tear from his eyes, and looked at Levi. "Have ya ever seen such a sight, son? This is what all the land was like before we came here. I reckon we be partly to blame. If we'd had any sense, as soon as we saw how delicate the balance of nature was up here, we should have gone home. Maybe if nobody ever came up here, things would be just as virgin as ten thousand years ago. This land hasn't changed in a heck of a long time. At least until now. Now, I'm afraid we're seeing the last days of the mountain man's glory."

"We better make the best of it," Levi whispered in a voice that could barely be heard. He didn't want to scare the buffalo. "Everything's perfect. This was the country I imagined back in Indiana as a boy."

"This right here is why I stayed on all those years ago," Dennis said. "It was worth it, too, wasn't it, Rusty?"

"It takes a man's breath away, don't it?" Rusty said. "I reckon we won't want for food this year." He laughed loud and hard. Levi was afraid he would spook the buffalo, but they continued to graze, oblivious to the hunters above them.

Levi closed his eyes and smelled. Buffalo's hide filled his senses. There was something else back there too, but he couldn't put a finger on it. That was when Dennis opened his eyes and locked eyes with Levi. They both smelled it, and it was sweat and buffalo fat.

"I reckon the Crow Indians have followed us this time," Dennis said. "Maybe we weren't as careful comin' up here as we should have been."

"Well, now that they know we're here and there's the buffs right in front of us, I reckon we can shoot enough for us at the compound and a bunch more for the Crow tribe. We can leave 'im to butcher as soon as we leave. I doubt they will come down and join us. They don't like White folks all that much. I can't say as I blame 'em either."

Levi quickly cut some branches down with his massive knife. It was big, but it matched his size. When in his hands, it appeared normal, but in the hands of others, it looked twice as big. He made three bipods to rest their guns on when they began to shoot. They buried them into the ground until they were as steady as a rock. Then they commenced shooting. The Crow watched in awe from a distance. The three men were the best shots in the compound, and Rusty and Levi were better than anyone they had ever seen. Both at shooting and reloading. Everything seemed to move in a well-lubricated movement. It was all smooth and calculated. Take a bead, fire, reload, and take another aim.

After the first hour, Crow Indians began to cover the valley floor where the buffalo lay dead and ready to butcher. The three mountain men continued to take down the estimated number of buffs to get the tribe and them through the winter and a bit more, just in case.

Indian children were sitting in the buffalo grass eating piping hot sweetbreads while the mothers and fathers toiled at taking every available part of the animals they butchered.

The sound of sliding rocks made the three snap around with their rifles following their eyes. They let out a sigh of relief when they saw it was Hachta. He was grinning like a jackal.

"This is a fine day, isn't it, Rusty Steel?" Hachta laughed. Rusty and Dennis joined in.

Once the fright from a Crow war chief sneaking up on them like it was nothing at all passed, Levi, too, began to chuckle. He made a note to work on his awareness skills some more. They weren't yet foolproof by a long sight.

They returned to their guns and bipods and continued to shoot until Rusty, Dennis, and Hachata agreed they had plenty to pass a well-fed winter. Nobody asked Levi's opinion or mentioned the strangeness of them working like this together. It was something Levi had never heard from them in everyday conversation or of an evening by the campfire. All three acted like they did it every day.

Levi couldn't help but have mixed feelings. He knew Hachta had sent several miners to their deaths for trespassing. This was something that Johnson found excessive, and he couldn't get his arms around the idea. It was so extreme. At the same time, he watched as the tribe's leader made one good choice after another for his people. He was wise, unlike the miners who came up the mountain or some settlers who went too far and paid with their lives.

Then his mind returned to the chore at hand, and he shot his last two buffalo. Rusty and Dennis also dropped two more each. Those were the extra animals to provide an additional stock of meat for somebody who dropped by the Crow camp for a visit, which was becoming more typical as time passed. There was a time when nobody came to these mountains. Only the local Indian tribes. Or they came to their compound, which was becoming normal, whether they liked it or not.

One minute the Crow war chief was standing

behind them, and the next, he was gone. They didn't even hear him leave. That was all three of them, and two were the epitome of mountain men.

Maybe I'll never know as much as an Indian, Johnson thought. *But I'm gonna try just the same.*

TEETH AND CLAWS

THE ALPHA MALE RACED THROUGH THE WILDERNESS WITH twenty more wolves snapping at his heels. They were all still hungry and only averaged half what they could eat in a day. They roamed the mountains ravenous for any prey, no matter the size or variety. Every poor animal in their path was killed and devoured so quickly it was like an eating machine hit them and spat out the bones. They riddled the trail with the remains of what they ate, both men and beasts.

Their last meal was the human. They had waited at the watering holes, but no elk or deer showed. The wolves were numerous and clever, too, making them dangerous. Of course, they couldn't reason, but their instincts were a complicated network that allowed them to subconsciously see where they were to go. They were automatically drawn to the smell of fresh blood. The powerful animals ran in leaps and bounds. The odd rabbit would jump from its shelter only to be snatched up by rabid jaws and devoured before it died. A fox made a mad dash for safety, but a single wolf broke off from the pack, easily outran the small canine, and broke its neck. It devoured it in minutes; then it ran after the rest of the pack and toward the smell of more blood. The little fox was skinny due to the lack of food. The whole food chain seemed affected, from the elk down. Nobody made it a serious habit to hunt grizzly bears, with a few exceptions. Most of them did it for the fun. The Indian warriors killed a grizzly to show they were worthy of their status.

They were all on the run, and now they all smelled the scent like the leader of their pack. The fact he smelled it so much sooner was proof of his superior skills. No male in the pack dared challenge him because they knew that if they lost, and they survived, they would be banned from the pack forever and would have to live the life of a lone wolf.

As the pack ran, if you saw them from above, they looked like a long snake. Each wolf had a place in the family. As they traveled the narrow trail at such speeds, they blurred into one long motion of black and gray hair. As they snaked up the switchback trails, a cloud of dust rose in their wake as they sped for their next meal.

They raced down the hill and up the other side. When they reached the top, their prey came into view. Two miners with a single mule were making their way down the mountain. They were paranoid as they held their rifles in their hands with white-knuckled fists. The two miners had heard about the Crow Indians snatching up stragglers, but they were two, and as far as they had heard, they were attacking one at a time. Then one miner thought about the people who were unaccounted for. Of course, they could have vanished in the night without telling the others where they were going.

Maybe they had found a gold strike worth it to them to remain in the Rockies.

These two miners were scared to death and wished they had never come to the mountains in the first place. They couldn't even explain why they had left their homes in such a rush without thinking things through. Before they knew it, they were in the Rocky Mountains with a bunch of fools who read the same newspaper article they had and believed it just like them. That was when they realized they had committed a folly for which they might pay with their lives.

They were the first to go back down the mountain, but they were so scared they moved at a snail's pace. They hid behind trees every few moments when they heard something rustle in the bushes. They thought they heard Indians everywhere they turned. They often stopped and backtracked because they thought they heard a human, a voice, or even when they thought they smelled sweat. They were so paranoid that if somebody snuck up behind them and said boo, they would probably jump out of their skin.

They had just burst into a run again as they made their way down and out of the mountains and to safety. They prayed for God to get them to home and swore they would never leave town again and go to church every Sunday. The second wannabe miner fingered a string of prayer beads as they rushed down. He was desperately pleading to the Heavens to save them. They never noticed the pack of wolves when they stopped at the top of the hill behind them. Forty eyes stared their way, but they never felt them either. They were about to find out they were in a place they should never have gone. Mother Nature was about to spring a surprise on them that would cost them their lives.

The lead wolf shifted its eyes across the land, looking for the perfect place to spring the trap. They instinctively knew these humans had the means to kill some of them but not enough. The lead wolf leaped up the steep rock wall and then sprang over to another cliff. He moved from stone to stone like he was half Billy goat. In seconds, they were above the men, and they dropped from the trees above, crashing down on their prey but never losing their balance. The men were on the ground before they realized they had been attacked.

If they were still standing, they might have had a chance to kill three or four and with some luck, maybe scare them off. But it happened so quickly, and from above, that they had no chance even to react. They were twenty ravished wolves' dinner. The sound of tearing flesh and growling animals blocked all smells of other creatures. Small animals ran for their lives now that the pack of wolves was busy with their prey.

In minutes, they were reduced to bones. Then they tore open the mule's neck. Soon, some of the wolves' heads disappeared into the belly of the large animal. It never made a sound, just like the men. The alpha wolf was more intelligent than their prey, and now they had another meal. This one was a little bigger, but they weren't full.

Blood dripped from white canine teeth and matted in blotches on their fur. Their eyes flashed green as they darted around, looking for signs of danger. Bones cracked between vice-like jaws, and long tongues slurped the bone marrow.

When they finished with the miners, they all turned

toward their leader. He sniffed the air again, turned, and ran through the rest of the day, looking for more prey. Hungry packs of wolves could cover thirty miles in a day. Night came, and still they roared through the forest. Finally, when they were all run out, they dropped where they stood and fell into a deep, exhausted sleep. Some wolves snored, and others dreamed as they moved their paws restlessly. They were probably dreaming about the two-legged game they had taken that day.

The wolves stirred as coyotes sang in the distance. The pack leader raised its snout and sniffed the air again. He could immediately smell blood, albeit ten miles away. He twitched his ears like ear trumpet horns, moving them as he picked out and separated every sound in the forest. He could hear the blare of a bull buffalo in the distance. The animal instantly knew there was a slaughter. The alpha male wolf stood and howled at the rising moon. The other wolves at his feet stirred, and all began to move as the leader ran off for the herd of buffalo. It instinctively knew this would feed them for days.

A wolf could survive two full weeks between meals but doing so made them mean. This pack had suffered a lack of food during the entire last month. As the pack instinctively grew to take down larger animals, they became brazen too. They no longer feared humans. Now, they would attack anything short of a full-grown grizzly bear. These wolves had raced across the mountain, killing every mammal in their path, but it was just enough to keep twenty canines on their feet. The alpha male knew he needed what he smelled, so he roared off after the scent of blood.

The leader suddenly made a sharp turn down a

steep cliff and sailed through the air, landing on all fours. It stopped as it snapped its head around, sniffing out its environment. The other wolves dropped at his feet. When they were all down, they shot off like bullets toward the smell of dead buffalo. The leader raced ahead of his pack, knowing the target would appear soon. It jumped off the path and raced through the brush. A wake of movement shook the leaves as he passed as fast as he could run. When they ran by, they were no more than a blur.

They burst into an even faster run as they came closer to the smell of death and blood. Now their bodies were sleek as they roared across the rugged land like it was a flat trail. The patter of dozens of feet was heard behind the leader as they ran for the fresh meat.

Levi was the first to see them when they raced onto the killing field. He was surprised at the size of the pack.

"Hey, Rusty. You see them wolves? Whatcha think we ought to do?"

Rusty Steel slowly loaded his gun and licked his thumb to wet the sight. Then he used the bipod to rest the heavy fifteen-pound barrel of the 54-caliber rifle. He moved the gunsight across the herd leading the wolves as they raced for the dead buffalo nearest to them. The Indian women worked on removing the hide were oblivious to their approach. The wolves were nearly on them when they turned and saw them.

Rusty took the shot, and the alpha male wolf dropped to the ground mortally wounded. The whole pack stopped and sniffed at the dead body of the pack's leader. Suddenly, two males started to fight, and the battle for the power of the next alpha male began. It lasted minutes as the mountain men watched and wondered what would happen next. All three men had their barrels pointed at the wolves nearest the Crow women.

Blood pumped out of his carotid artery. The winner snapped its jaws around its neck and applied pressure until it ceased to move. The new leader was wounded from the fight and limped off the killing fields. Now, the wolves didn't feel so confident with the humans. They had killed their leader, and their new alpha male was badly wounded. Only time would tell if the new leader survived his wounds or if there would be yet another fight for control. All the males were rivals. Three more shots came inbound, but they weren't meant to kill, although one bullet did nick the new leader's ear. It immediately turned for the forest and ran. It limped away weary and confused. They decided they would prefer to be hungry than dead. The whole pack of wolves followed him as they disappeared into the forest.

BUFFOONS

"Come on, Jed," Phil whispered. "These hillbillies that live up here ain't gonna catch us. Even if they do, what are they gonna do to a couple of chicken egg thieves? I doubt it's a hangin' offense." He laughed and slapped his hand over his mouth to stifle the sound. "Maybe we'll even get us a hen for supper." His shoulders shook as he continued to snicker silently.

"Yeah, and just maybe we'll get shot and kilt for a couple of measly eggs," Jed replied. "Even a chicken ain't worth dying over. Plus, who knows what those mountain men will do to us if they catch us? From what I hear, they make up their own laws as they go and don't adhere to the laws of the US government. Like they have special rights of their own. Don't that take the cake?"

"You believe too much of that rubbish you read in the city newspapers," Phil said. "I say none of them men can read a lick, and they're as dumb as a salt lick. I've talked to one or two, and in my experience, they aren't much more than heathens with a few pieces of White man's clothes. The ones I met you could hardly understand. I reckon the majority of them have Injun blood, or the Crow would have already killed them. How else would they survive where White men can't? The sooner we get off this dad-gummed mountain, the better for me. It can't be soon enough."

Jed suddenly stopped, and Phil bumped into him, making them both stumble and fall to the ground with their faces in the dirt.

"Watch where you're going, fool," Phil spat. "You might have broken my arm. Look where you're going, would ya."

"I was lookin' where I was goin'," Jed whispered, angry. "That's why I stopped, you moron. The cabins are right there. Lucky for us, we've got a fair bit of moon tonight. We'll be in and back out in two minutes. It'll take those hillbillys that long even to wake up and pull them Indian moccasins on they wear. From what I hear, most of 'em are usually deep into their whiskeys, so they'll probably be sleeping one off. I've read the articles about the Rendezvous, and it sounds like one drunken festival that lasts a couple of weeks. Can you imagine being drunk for that long?"

They walked around the outside of the zig-zag post fence as they headed for the gate. Phil carefully slipped the loop over the gatepost and opened it just enough for them to slip by. He hooked the loop back in place so it wouldn't swing open. Then they made a beeline for the chicken coop—white feathers showed silver on the ground in the moonlight. They were littered all over. He stopped and looked around before he headed for the door.

"Make sure you don't make any noise," Phis said.

"We don't want to wake 'im up. I wonder how many fellas live in the three cabins?"

"Hush up now, or they're gonna hear ya runnin' off at the mouth," Jed snapped.

They carefully made their way toward the chicken house. He could hear a few clucks inside, but most of the hens were asleep. The smell of chickens filled their senses. Jed imagined a couple of fried eggs. He was as hungry as he'd ever been. He could almost smell them and feel the grease leap out of the frying pan. Maybe they would take a dozen if there were that many. Why steal two when you can steal ten? When they came to the door, it was closed. It had a latch, but there was no lock on it. Jed pulled at the door, but it resisted.

He looked around, grabbed the handle with both hands, and gave it a good jerk. As soon as the door opened, a large brass bell above it rang like a fire station. It scared the daylight of Phil, but it fell from the top of the door onto Jed's head and knocked him out cold. Suddenly men with torches surrounded them. They had fallen into a trap. They stared down several gun barrels, and behind them were angry faces. The flames made shadows flicker on the mountain men, simultaneously making them all the more mysterious and dangerous. Phil peed himself as Jed lay at his feet.

Little did they know everybody in the compound expected the miners to hit the chicken house when they headed back down the mountain—at least those who had made it out alive. Nobody knew how many survived and how many perished. Actually, nobody even knew how many miners there were in in the first place. So, Forrester once again used his smarts and thought of the alarm bell. He took it down from Dennis's porch and hung it above the door of the chicken shed. That's why the door was so hard to open. The big chunk of brass fell right on Jed's head.

"Howdy, fellas," Phil said with a false smile, but the truth lay in his frightened eyes. "We were just gonna go over to the porch and knock on the door to see if anybody was home."

"And you were gonna do this in the middle of the night?" Rusty Steel growled with a knife in his hand. "It's past midnight, fool. Do you know what we do with chicken thieves?" He held the blade up as the flames glinted off the shiny steel.

"Why, we weren't doing nothing, mister," Phil replied, trying to be too friendly. "We're just two of them miners the Indians run off the mountain, that and a bunch of wolves. We were gonna come and ask y'all to sell us a few eggs. Ain't that right, Jed?"

"Wolves?" Levi asked. "Ya don't say."

"And these wolves chased ya right to our cabins and to the door of the chicken house?" Dennis asked. "I reckon they were after all the chickens and even our rooster, and you were just trying to do us a neighborly favor and stop 'im before they got the door open. Is that what you're tryin' to tell us? You were tryin' to hold the chicken coop door closed? And where are these wolves now? I don't even see a dog. If y'all came to buy eggs ya must have brought money? So, show us the money and we'll sell ya some eggs. Or were ya really after our hens?"

"We were only gonna steal a couple of eggs," Phil said it before he realized his mistake. He had thoughtlessly blabbered their guilt.

"How long do you think it'll take his partner to come around?" Levi asked.

"I'm surprised it knocked him out," Forrester said. "It only fell from the top of the door, but it was mighty heavy. I hope it didn't kill him. Then we couldn't hang these two by the neck like we'd planned."

Jed was finally coming around, and Phil was just about to faint and join him on the ground. His head spun as he searched for a way out of a bad situation. When he heard the word hanged, he panicked. When the tall blond-haired fellow said it, he didn't doubt him a moment. He said it so full of confidence, like it was already a done deal.

I'll be able to talk my way out of this little mess with these hillbillies, Phil thought. *No problem.*

"You're a sneaky bunch," Phil spat. "Tricking innocent folks and all. We be good people. Maybe it's you folks who are the wolves, and we are but the lambs."

"But not a minute ago, you said you came here to steal eggs," Rusty replied. "So which is it? Did you come here to read the Bible with us, or did you come for the chickens?"

"Get the rope, Levi," Dennis said. "I don't like to diddle about. When ya got something to do, it's best to get to it."

Jed sat in the dirt with his head in his hands. He had yet to realize what was happening. He moaned as blood ran from his scalp and down his neck. It was just a small flesh wound, though.

Before the two knew it, they had slipped lassos around their ankles, and suddenly they were flying off the ground and into the air like they were big ugly birds. They flailed their arms and yelled as the mountain men laughed. Jed still hadn't recuperated from the bang on the head and passed out again. Phil wiggled around like a beached trout. His mouth opened and closed as he gobbled up air.

———

OUT IN THE night at the now vacant miner's camp stood a single Indian—he was the only one to remain. He sat on one of the rocks Rex and Cid had chosen to watch the circus that played out before them. The Indian wondered if the men who lived in this tent had survived. Had they made their escape down the mountain or had they been the ones brought back to his camp?

He had also seen the massive pack of wolves and the bones of two men. Had they not been dressed, he would never have been able to tell if they were Indian or White men. But their clothing gave them away. The miners he found didn't have a chance of survival. As soon as such a large pack split a single person off, they would quickly have them for their next meal. This wasn't new in the Rockies, but it was unusual that the pack was so big. Usually, packs ran in groups of five to nine with the biggest one being fifteen strong at the very most, and that was very unusual.

This was the largest pack of wolves Hachta had ever seen. Of course, they had heard lies of packs of a hundred. Just like grizzlies, the campfire exaggerated everything. Indeed, this story would be told time and time again, and each time it would change, like a caterpillar into a butterfly.

As he sat, fires danced in his eyes—they were from the flames of the miners' tents. When they ran them all off, they hadn't allowed them to take their lodges, so they would have no homes to return with. That's what they would do to an Indian enemy. The entire camp was ablaze. It went up like a kerosene-soaked cloth. Flying pieces of flaming tents flew through the air like burning birds. Black smoke rose into the sky. Hachta nodded with approval. The thick smoke would tell everyone who saw it the story, and they would be warned not to come and take the yellow mineral or hunt their game.

Hachta would have to remember to send out a hunting party to hunt down the wolves. Now that they had killed humans, they were man-killers and had to die. If he wanted to protect his people, he had to remember to see they were stopped. Usually, they forgave wolves for their indiscretions. Many believed the Indian people came from wolves, or some of their gods were wolves, so they usually didn't hunt them. They often turned the young wolf-pups they found into Indian camp dogs. They were intelligent, obedient, and vicious if a stranger got near their camp.

Hachta remembered back to seeing the massive herd of buffalo. He smiled at the thought. He felt it would be one of the last massive herds he would ever see. He cherished each time he saw such wonder and stood in awe. He still had to get to know the two new young men before deciding whether he would allow them to stay or make them go—just like he did with the other six men who lived on Crow land. They were valuable to them at the moment because that is where they traded for steel tools like hatchets and hammers. Also, for gunpowder for the few rifles they owned.

The women liked the mirrors and Italian beads. They also had mother-of-pearl inlaid hairbrushes. The women had never seen such things and soon had become accustomed to possessing these White man's luxuries. If he were to send the eight mountain men away, they would be angry with the war chief. Maybe the chief would admonish him for his indiscretions. As long as they had their value to the Crow tribe, they could stay. At least the first six. Time would tell what would happen to the other two.

For the moment, there had been enough excitement for one season. Maybe one day, he would invite Rusty Steel to live with them when he decided it was time to run the others off. He didn't expect it to be too long. All the fools that came up here to look for gold were only a taste of what was to come. He was smart enough to know the White men would continue to come in more significant numbers every time. He believed the Crow Nation would cease to exist when they filled the land with their wooden homes and wagons.

The clock was ticking for the Plains Indians, and they knew they were running out of time. This year, they were lucky because the mountain men found an isolated buffalo herd. He didn't know how they did it, but it saved them many problems during the coming winter. That and Rusty was clever enough to kill a number of buffalo for the tribe to have meat for the winter. He knew only one mountain man like him. He wondered if the two new men were like Rusty Steel or if they were like Dennis and the others?

His people had come and butchered enough buffalo meat for the winter, and some extra if friendly tribes needed food. They only took from the herd what they needed to replace homes with buffalo skins and to fill their families' bellies. Everyone feasted on large steaks that evening. Everybody in the tribe was happy, which wasn't as common a thing as one would think. It was a difficult job for a war chief to keep the camp safe and the chief happy. He wondered how hard it would be to have the responsibility of chief.

He chuckled. The women of his tribe loved Angus when he danced. He was always invited to the powwows. He had forgotten how many wives he had. He believed it was more than four. Maybe he, too, could stay when the day came. He was married to a Crow Indian, and Green Leaves would be very angry if he didn't at least offer him the chance to continue to live on their mountain—but in their camp. He knew one day he would have to burn the cabins. They were symbols of change, and that was something the Crow Indians couldn't allow.

All White man seemed to think about was change while Indians thought about important things like traditions. He knew their ways would vanish and maybe even the name of their tribes would cease to be spoken. Then they would truly disappear from the plains, like many had before them.

Hachta doubted this time would be in the too distant future because things were changing much faster than he expected. He could see the difference in the last five years. The Rendezvous was a perfect example. At first, a few mountain men attended. But the last event was well over five hundred participants, and they were all drunk and fought in the streets. Their presence brought women who sold their bodies for money by the hour. He knew in coming years they would come in the thousands. One day they would have to move their camp.

He continued to sit as he watched the flames. He pulled out a ceramic pipe Rusty Steel had given him. He filled it with a tobacco twist. He stuck a branch in the tent burning next to him and lit the pipe. As smoke billowed around his head, his face glowed orange from the cinders.

TOMORROW

"WHATCHA THINK, DARLIN'?" ANGUS MCFARLIN ASKED his Crow wife. "Are any more of those miners wandering around out there that we should know about? If they've all gone down the mountain, we can rest easy and go wherever we want. I might take Green Leaves back to her village. It's been too hectic here of late."

"The few that are still on the mountain are near their departure from this world," Green Leaves said as she stared into space. "They will be in their spirit world soon if they aren't already there. They were not many, so there will be no problems from the Army. Hachta was smart and didn't make too many people pay for the injustice. If only White men were as fair as the Crow, we would no longer have problems. The problem with White men is they like to own land. They make pieces of paper that say this land is theirs, then throw the original owners off. How long have White men been in America? We Indians have been here for ten thousand years."

"I believe it won't take humans nearly as long to destroy everything," Forrester said. "I think if we keep on going like we are, we'll be a killin' machine soon enough—slaughtering everything that defies us. I'm glad I'm no longer a soldier. I will only kill an Indian if he tries to kill me, and I will do so regretfully. When I reflect on what the Army has already done and what is to come, I get chills up my spine."

"Ain't life funny like that," Rusty said. "No time ago, you were all gung-ho ready to take on the entire Comanche Nation and any other tribe that dared challenge you and your fancy white horse. You still wear that hat slapped up on the side when a fur cap would do ya better. You refuse to allow what happened to sink into your mind. You're just tryin' to hold on to somethin' that ain't there anymore. Now that you've grown out of playing soldier boy, you can become a real man. A mountain man like your pard here, Levi."

"I figure Forrester is already a mountain man, too," Levi said, standing up for his buddy. "I've heard you say it anyway. I think he's every bit as much a mountain man as I am or will ever be." Even when he said it, he knew it wasn't true and would never be, but just the same, Will was his friend, and he felt he had to defend him.

"Well, son," Rusty said. "There're mountain men, and there're mountain men. He'd pass anywhere but in the Rocky Mountains. Here you need a bit more of the knowledge to get the honor of carrying the name like a badge on your chest. But don't you worry. He's coming along just fine. I believe the loss of that arm might have been the best thing ever happened to ya, William. That's what your folks called ya, didn't they? Yeah, I reckon you come from a place that's just about as far away from here as a man can get. That's why it's a tad harder for ya, but when ya get there, it'll have all the more merit."

"I never thought about it like that," Forrester said. "If the truth is known, when I look back, I can see I thought I was riding on my high horse, prancing around like a rooster. I did think I knew everything, like I was accused of. Now, I find that I'm just beginning to know myself, let alone think I'm a know-it-all."

"Age and a little maturing will do that to ya every time." Angus laughed. They all laughed, even Forrester. "Look at me. I don't rightly know how old I am, but I've never completely grown up. All you have to do is be around when I cut the rug." He grinned so wide you could see his tonsils.

"What are your people gonna do to the White folks they captured?" Levi asked Green Leaves. "I imagine it'd be too much to ask your chief to spare their lives."

"What does the White man do when men disobey the tribes' rules?"

"In the Army, we put them before a firing squad," Forrester said. He saw she was puzzled. "We shoot them."

"The city folks hang 'im," Angus said. "I seen a hangin' once, but I don't wanna see another. It was like a circus had come to town, with folks sellin' everything from elixirs to hair-growin' lotion. But it was an ugly sight once they got on with the deal and hung the horse thief. It took the fella the longest time to stop kickin' about. I'd rather get 'et by a grizzly bear."

"I wonder how many were in that pack of wolves?" Levi asked. "I bet they killed more than a couple Crow huntin' buffalo. I've never seen nothin' like that back in southwestern Indiana. They could take down a half dozen men if they took a mind. I figure out here, Mother Nature is the biggest killer of men who aren't Indians. Maybe even the Indians too. Life up here is mighty hard at times. Then again, that's part of the beauty. It's the feeling a man can survive in such conditions in exchange for living in God's gift to humankind. The earth and all its glory. We live in one of the most beautiful places in the world. Of course, that comes with a price, like everything of true value."

Rusty stared at Levi for a moment before speaking. "Sometimes you surprise me with how fast you learn, son. It's almost uncanny the way you absorb so much of your surroundings. Things that a man like me can't teach a man like you. You have to learn all alone, but you're getting your arms around things I took years to do. Soon, we'll be followin' you when we go out to hunt. By golly, we already are sometimes. It'll lift a load off my shoulders if I know you can take up where I left off."

"Why don't you stop tryin' to make everything about you, Rusty?" Angus growled. "Of course, the boy's smarter and a better tracker than you. By now, I bet he's a better shot, too, not to mention he's better lookin' and twice as big. I don't know what you see in your mind that makes you think so much of yourself. You must have some grand picture of Rusty Steel locked away in that sick brain of yours, but I can guarantee that none of us see it, including me."

"I did grow up in the wild." Levi grinned. "I reckon I've been training for this moment my entire life. Now that I've got this far, I'm just beginnin' to realize how much more I still have to learn."

"I reckon you have," Rusty said and smiled—it

reached his eyes. "As I said, I can pick 'em out, can't I, Angus?"

"I've never heard a man compliment himself so much as you." Dennis laughed. "That's why I never say anything nice to ya, Rusty. If I added to your ego, your head might burst."

"Go ahead and laugh, fool," Rusty growled. "You'll never be half the mountain man I am. Why, you can't even shoot compared to me."

"We ain't comparin' me to you." Dennis cackled. "We're comparin' you to Levi. The one you say you're teaching everything you know. Heck, he already knows twice that of you, old fool."

"And you tell us we act like children," Forrester said. "You all act more like kids than we ever do. Look at cha, arguing about everything under the sun."

"Now you've done it." Angus laughed. "You've done insulted the high and mighty Master Steel. I doubt his ego will tolerate it."

"Ain't you done with that sign yet, Angus?" Rusty grumbled. "You started making it before we left on the last hunt."

"I just finished," Angus replied as he smiled and showed them what he had painted. He blew on the black paint and turned it around for everyone to see.

It said: *NO TRESPASSING for two-legged and four-legged critters. That means humans, horses, mules, and pigs. This ain't a restaurant or a hotel, so don't stop and try to visit because you won't be welcomed with open arms. Instead, you'll have your backsides filled with rock salt from a scatter-gun, signed: by the Compound Manager, Angus McFarlin.*

"No wonder you took so long to make the sign." Forrester laughed. "It's as long as a book."

"So, now you're the compound manager, are ya?" Dennis asked. "And who gave you such a title? I was the first one here, so I should have a say so in who is who."

"Why, because that's my job—it always has been," Angus said, surprised at the challenge. "I'm the diplomat to keep the peace with the Indians, and I'm better at sign language and smoke signals than any of y'all. I know more about Indians than all of ya combined. Now, you tell me why I'm not the most qualified for the job. My writing is even pretty. Some of you old farts still can't even sign your name."

"Don't put me in that bunch," Rusty said. "It's me that always reads to y'all when we got a newspaper. Once upon a time, I was a ship captain."

"You mean once upon a time, you were a river rat." Dennis laughed. "That's what you were as a boy, and you still got the stink on ya."

"The only reason we let ya read to us is so you'll shut your trap and stop talkin' all the time." Angus chuckled. "At least when you readin' to us, it's like somebody else is talkin' instead of you, and it ain't the same thing over and over again."

"I have a mind to go back to civilization and get me a woman and leave all of you up here with the crazy people who populate this here mountain," Rusty said.

"I think that's a fine title for ya, Angus," Levi said. He liked the tall gangly man with the Indian wife. He thought he had a lot to learn from even him. "You sure as heck are the ambassador with the Indians, and nobody can say different."

"Now we got the youngsters givin' us wise old men their opinions." Angus laughed. He loved provoking Rusty, and he was baiting the two new clan members to see if they would bite too. "The next thing you know, Levi will be telling us what to do, and Forrester there will have us wearing uniforms. Up and at 'em at five o'clock in the morning. I'm sorry to tell y'all, but that ain't gonna ever happen."

The tent city no longer existed. The Indians and the wind had swept away the last signs of their presence. At least with the coming freezing temperatures, no strangers would dare venture into the mountains again until summer. Now, the mountain men would have a few months ahead of them with no visitors—and even better, no trespassers—interrupting their solitude.

Levi wondered if Dennis and the others lived in the other cabins just to keep a little distance from Rusty Steel. He was a handful, but all the joking aside, they all knew he was the best mountain man of the bunch. It was just because he made sure everybody knew about it that they felt they had to poke fun at him. These were their customs, and nobody saw a change in the future.

The only indication that the gold fever-stricken people were ever there was the smell of the ashes of dead fires. Somewhere in a Crow camp, captives screamed for mercy, but the Indians could show none, or more would come from where they came. Then they would have to move their camp somewhere White people hadn't yet reached. They disapproved of the Indians' ways and wanted to change their lives for something called progress and civilization. Neither sounded promising for the Indian Nations.

The miners' tools lay abandoned, with no owners left to use them. Not a creature was in sight except the birds. They provided a symphony. The rumble of water falling into a still pond could be heard in the background.

In the crystal-clear lagoon, a fish swam lazily across the bottom. A lizard climbed a tree seeking the sun's warmth. A light breeze ruffled the leaves. Cicadas turned off and on again like a switch. The old oak's roots crawled across the earth to the bank's edge. Rays of light refracted through the water, lighting up the bottom. Something else sparkled there among the sand. Gold dust shined where it washed down from the crevice in the mountains. Maybe there was gold in the Rocky Mountains after all. Lucky for everybody, nobody had found it.

OUTLAWS

LEVI JOHNSON MOUNTAIN MAN SCOUT 6

This book is dedicated to the Enriquez sisters, Cinta, Maribel, Lola, and Nines.

There are only two ways to live your life. One is as though nothing is a miracle. The other is as though everything is a miracle.

Albert Einstein

OUTLAWS

It was Sunday, and as usual, everybody was on Rusty Steel's front porch, just finishing breakfast. It was Angus's turn to cook. Since they'd gone from two to four people living in the cabin, they decided to rotate the basic chores. Each one would cook breakfast and supper, and everybody sorted out lunch for themselves. Their midday meal usually consisted of a stale biscuit and some hard tack. Often, they were miles away from the cabin for their noon meal.

They had plenty of food stock, and the traps were ready for the season, but Levi wanted to have a look for some new streams and beaver dams. Now that the supply appeared to be dwindling, Johnson decided to take it upon himself to explore a bit farther into the wilderness, looking for new locations to set traps. Levi had grown up trapping and was an expert from his youth back home in southwestern Indiana, where he was known as the Trapper Boy. He even had traps of his own invention. He was always looking for ways to improve things too.

"Today, Will and I are gonna ride out past your old string of traps and look deeper in the forest for places harder to find and reach," Levi said. "Maybe that will make up for the lack of beaver on this side of the mountain. If the wild game is gettin' scarce, I imagine it'll be the same with the beaver."

"That ain't a bad idea," Rusty said. "Iffin ya want, I can ride along and show you all the spots we've trapped in the past, then we can follow the streams farther up the mountain."

Angus went around the table, doling out cups of coffee from a gallon kettle. Steam bubbled from the spout as the air filled with the smell of java.

Dennis cocked his head and sniffed the air. Before he could speak, they heard horses' hooves hammering the earth as riders neared. Levi pulled his pistols from his belt and cocked the hammers. He lay them before him on the table, ready were they necessary. Will sat beside him. One jacket sleeve was folded and empty. With his other hand he tapped the grip of his pistol in his britches and waited. The pounding came louder until two horses came into sight. They were riding recklessly fast for the narrow mountain trail. Both riders snapped looks behind them as they fled. They rode so fast that they almost rode right by Rusty's cabin. When they saw them on the porch, one of the riders pulled up to such a sharp stop the horse nearly sat down.

Both men wore remnants of uniforms of Union soldiers, and they were armed. Rifles were strapped over their shoulders, and pistols hung from their saddle horns. They wore Army-issue boots and britches. Both horses had US ARMY brands burned into their skin.

Ex-Captain Forrester watched as a bad feeling began

to eat at his stomach. He took his hat off and set it on the vacant chair. Will waited to see what the fleeing soldiers were doing way the hell up here with winter knocking at their door. Obviously, something more dangerous than the weather was after them. Their horses' lungs sounded like steam engines and sweat glistened on their hides. Both men's eyes were spread wide, and their jaws ground their teeth.

They wheeled their horses around and raced up to the porch.

"Whoa, whoa, whoa, there now," Rusty called out as he stood. He, too, had his hand on the grip of his pistol. "Who gave you two permission to ride into our compound?"

"I'm plumb sorry, mister, but we've got bounty hunters on our trail. My name is Todd Zillow, and my partner's Jimmy Jones. I'm afraid we're deserters. I'm gonna be honest with y'all. We've been fightin' Indians for the last year, but things went wrong south of Old Fort Boise. Captain Holmes ordered our patrol to massacre a bunch of old men, women, and children. When we refused the lieutenant's orders, he went to shoot us for disobeying, and I shot and killed the fool. I ain't gonna murder any more Indians."

"Our government put a bounty on our heads for desertion in a time of war, but there ain't no war—with the local Indians, it's a bloody massacre. But now we're wanted for murder, just the same," Jimmy huffed. "But it was kill or be killed. I'd swear to that on a Bible. We had no choice, mister. Still, the Army sent men after us just the same."

"You mean the Indian wars, which've been raging for ten years or more," Will said.

"The captain and the marshal intend to collect our bounties," Todd said.

The privates gave Will a fleeting glance, but their eyes bounced around like marbles in a tin can, and they didn't notice his Army-issue boots. His saber hung on the wall inside the cabin over the fireplace out of sight.

"Since when are Army captains bounty hunters?" Angus asked, confused. "Sure, I can see 'im comin' after y'all, but the Army don't pay soldiers bounties, as far as I know."

"I doubt they'd follow us so far into the mountains iffin it wasn't for the bounty," Todd said. "The Army will come after us, no doubt, but that will happen in the spring when they don't risk getting stuck up in the mountains when the first snows hit. That's why we came here, thinking nobody in their right mind would follow us. But that ain't the case. They were close enough when we hit the base of the mountain; we could see one wore a badge like a marshal or something. The other one was Captain Holmes."

"I doubt a sheriff would leave his town to come after us," Jimmy said. "Plus, we shot the lieutenant in the wilderness at the Sioux camp while looking for war parties. Holmes figured if we murdered their families, they would come looking for us, and he would set up an ambush, but James and I didn't want anything to do with it. We figured we could hide out for the winter; then, in the spring, we would head for California, where we ain't known, and change our names. I hear lots of outlaws from places like Kansas go west to escape the law."

The men on the porch sat silent. They'd thought they would have a quiet winter after the mess with the miners. The pack of wolves was still out there roaming around, looking for their next meal. The prolonged silence began to eat at the two soldiers. They wanted the mountain men to say something, but they were as mute as a tree stump.

Finally, Will asked, "How far is this captain behind you men?"

Todd blinked his eyes and stared at the blond man with blue eyes. His voice held authority, but Todd couldn't figure out why.

"I doubt they be more than half a day behind us if not a few hours," Todd replied. "Moving into the mountains and leaving the trails has put them off, and they have to track us now. Hopefully, it'll slow 'em down until they get tired and turn back. We ain't gonna stop runnin' until we lose 'em, or we're someplace where they can't touch us."

"If you stand there jawing all day, I imagine the bounty hunters will find you soon enough," Rusty said. His eyes were full of mischief, but the soldiers were too scared to notice.

"Yes, sir," Todd said.

He didn't even know why he stopped. He figured it was because he was scared. These friendly gentlemen couldn't fix his problem, though. Todd knew he was right, and they had to keep running, or they would begin to gain on them. "If you see the captain, I'd appreciate it if you didn't tell him you saw us."

"But we did see ya, and we ain't the type of men to lie," Rusty said. "You best run along now. You're wasting daylight, son."

With blank eyes and pale faces, they wheeled their

horses around, rode out of the compound, and then charged up the trail.

"If they keep pushing those horses like that, soon they'll be afoot," Dennis said. "Mind you, the first thing I would have done was got rid of those Army horses. Just stealin' 'em is a hanging offense. Those boys got themselves into quite a mess."

"I'd hate to see what they do to 'im when they catch 'im," Levi said. "You can hardly blame 'im for not wantin' to kill elders, women, and children."

"Sometimes life's that way," Rusty said. "One thing goes wrong, and suddenly you find yourself in a whirl-wind, and no matter what you do, ya can't get out. It just keeps getting worse and worse."

Nobody noticed how the blood had drained from Will Forrester's face. He knew exactly how these two deserters felt. He had done something similar, only he hadn't shot one of his men. But still, he could see how it could happen. Some men had good hearts and weren't up to the atrocities the Army ordered them to commit. If someone pointed a gun at him, ready to shoot, he, too, would return fire. Nobody would stand there and allow themselves to be shot if they had any way around it.

He thought he had made a mess, but the two privates had it much worse. He couldn't see any way out of it for them unless they managed to vanish and survive a winter in the mountains. Only if they made it to California did they have a chance. If a captain and a marshal were willing to come into the Rocky Mountains to give chase, their bounty would be substantial.

Forrester knew how things went out of skew in the wilderness, so now he wondered if he would somehow, too, be chased for his desertion. Of course, he had written a letter of resignation, but he knew he should have returned to Fort Leavenworth to hand it in. Instead, he had sent it with his sergeant. He wondered if they made it or if they also perished on their return across the dangerous lands of Kansas and beyond. He somehow knew that wasn't the case, but the thought lingered. There were no guarantees west of St. Louis.

"I wonder if the two men chasing them will come by here too," Forrester said. "I'm not too keen on Army types anymore—not after all the trouble with the Comanche. Now I see things in a different light too. I know we're throwing the Indians off their land. There was a time when I was a part of it, but I had my fill too."

"Yeah, but you didn't shoot your superior officer," Rusty said. "There ain't no gettin' around that one. What you did was realize who you were and your path in life wasn't in the Army like you had believed. I doubt you know exactly what that implies but I can assure I don't know either."

"I did all the rest," Will whispered. "Even my horse was from the Army, just like those boys. I just kept him because nobody else could ride him. Now, I see my departure from the Army was full of holes."

"Maybe this morning we ought to have something stronger than sugar in our coffee," Angus said as he set a jug of corn liquor on the table.

Will grabbed the bottle, removed the cork, and poured a good dose. His hand shook, and his voice cracked when he said, "Maybe I ought to head on out for a spell. Iffin the Army is up here looking for desert- ers, I might just get caught up in this mess."

"You'll do no such thing," Rusty said. "The law has no say-so here in our compound. They might think they have, but they don't. A lot of men have come up here and never returned. We watch after our own."

Rusty Steel had always been wishy-washy with Will in the past. It was clear he hadn't decided if he would allow him to stay on for good or not. Will had thought Rusty would take a few months to decide, but it sounded more like he included him as one of them with what he just said. It gave Forrester a vote of confidence and a boost of morale.

"You just make sure you keep your mouth shut iffin they do come this way," Mountain Dennis said. "Marshals normally ain't too bad unless you get one that was an outlaw before he turned to the law. There's a good bit of that goin' on. The Army captain won't be havin' any distractions, though. He'll be one hundred percent invested in the hunt and most likely will have orders, meaning he won't turn back."

"I always do the talkin' for the group when something like this pops up," Rusty said. "It shouldn't affect us none, but you just never know. Up here, things can change as quickly as the direction of the wind."

They sat all morning, and Angus made some biscuits when lunchtime came around since they had nothing to do but wait. He also made strips of fried bacon to slap between the buns. The cook opened the first cast iron frying pan, and steam rose from the freshly cooked scones.

They sat in comfortable silence, everybody but Forrester. He was so antsy that he couldn't stay still. He had pulled his Army boots off and changed into a pair of buckskin pants Levi had laying around. He decided it was time to give up the last traces of his Army clothing. He had never thought about it before, but he should have. It had never even dawned on him that his commanding officers might send someone to detain him and bring him back. He wondered if the Army captain was after more than just those two.

A sudden urge sent him rushing for the corral. If this captain did pass by this way, he didn't want him to see the brand on his white stallion. That, too, carried the mark of the Army. Forrester had to tell himself not to panic, but his mind was spinning out of control. All the guilt of the expedition came back to the surface like the hot kiss at the end of a wet fist. All of the men he had lost to the attacks by the Comanche war party. They were the last thing he had expected on his journey.

He had wanted to do that expedition more than anything in the world. He knew he was on shaky ground when he left West Point and requested a posting in one of the frontier posts. At that point, he'd had no contact with wild Indians other than the dime novels he read. When the possibility had arisen for him to map out the land for future forts, he jumped at the chance.

He never doubted for a moment that they would make it across. Of course, he expected to have one or two hiccups on the way. The reality was they had bumps and potholes in the road all the way and lost half the expedition, including its most important member, the professor.

He roped his stallion and led him into the stables at the very end. Now, Mister Paranoia sat perched on his shoulder and was gnawing away at his brain. When he returned to the porch, he kept his eyes down, avoiding eye contact with his friends. The appearance of the two deserters had brought everything he had run away from back to him and smacked him right in the face. He wondered if the captain and marshal would really come, and when would they get there?

Levi sat on the porch puffing on his ceramic pipe as he stared at the trail leading to the cabin. Rusty whittled on a stick like he didn't particularly care if they came by his place or not. Nobody ruled over the men who lived in his compound, no matter what they thought. He knew it would be impossible to bring enough men and weapons to defeat them in their fortress-like building. Back in the day, they had spent years fighting off Indian attacks, so it would be their bread and butter every day.

THE LAW

THE POUNDING HOOVES THEY ALL EXPECTED TO HEAR grew louder by the second. A cloud of dust corkscrewed behind the two riders. Sunlight flashed off the tin star on one man's chest. The other wore the uniform of an Army captain. A saber hung on his left side. His graying mass of hair was pushed back on his head. His face was burned from days in the sun. His hat strap hung from one of the pistols in his belt.

They stormed up to the gate, the captain struggling with his big bay. It stomped its hooves in nervous anticipation. It was a war horse. A scar ran from the captain's cat-green eyes to his chin. A four-day stubble populated his face. Both men had dust in the wrinkles of their clothing and their skin. The captain spat into the dirt before he spoke.

"Permission to enter, gentlemen?" he asked. "I'm Captain Frank Holmes, and this is Marshal Jack Wilson."

"All right then," Angus said as he eyed the strangers. They walked their horses to the hitching rail and then went to dismount. Eight pairs of eyes stared hard at the strangers.

Eight rifles were lined up against the building, and a half dozen pistols were on the tabletop. Bone handles of long knives stuck from the men's boots and moccasins.

"Are you gentlemen expecting company?" Captain Holmes asked, raising his eyebrows. He eyed the weapons. It looked like they had been waiting on them.

"Nobody said nothin' about steppin' down. State your business, gentlemen, and make it snappy," Rusty said. "We've got chores to get on with."

"And to whom am I speaking?" the captain retorted.

"That's a fool question," Rusty retorted. "You're talkin' to *me*. You're the stranger here, so state your business—please, Captain."

The officer harrumphed and said, "We're huntin' two dangerous outlaws. They're wanted for several offenses to man and some to the Almighty. They're deserters, among other things."

"Why in the world would such a big army send one officer to hunt down two desperate outlaws?" Rusty asked. "I can see a marshal wanderin' around in the wilderness but not an Army captain all on his lonesome."

"I'm on a stay of leave," the captain replied. "The marshal is along to make it legal. Now that I've clarified my purpose, have you seen two soldiers ride this way in the last day? I doubt they are very far ahead of us."

"Hold on, now," Rusty said. "I may not be as bright as you, so give me a second to understand. You're wearin' the uniform of an Army officer, but you're not on duty. And you're chasing two deserters who you say have committed crimes against man and the Almighty both?"

"I reckon that makes you a bounty hunter, don't it?" Dennis said. "How much are you payin' the lawman?"

"Are you going to answer my question or not?" Captain Holmes spat. "I won't tolerate insubordination."

Rusty's feathers had just got rustled, and he growled, "Who in tarnation do you think you're talkin' to, fool? We're mountain men, not privates in your invisible army. Iffin I were you, I'd speak in a friendlier tone, or you might make one of my pards here angry."

Levi stood, making the officer's eyes rise to the porch roof. He saw a giant six feet seven inches tall and two hundred forty pounds of muscle, and he wasn't smiling.

"I've chopped bigger men than you down to size," the captain hissed like a snake in the grass. "If you don't answer my questions, you will suffer the consequences. I represent the United States Army and all the power behind it."

"You keep talkin about this big army you've got like it's right here, but I've yet to see soldier one." Levi smiled. "Up here, we live by our own set of laws. If I were you, I'd be careful not to break one. You're the one trespassing here, not us, so maybe you should tread carefully."

"What is the matter with you people?" Captain Holmes asked. "Do you want dangerous outlaws crawling all over your mountain, breaking up your peace and quiet?"

"The only one makin' a racket is you with all your jaw waggin'," Rusty grumbled. "Just because we're Americans don't mean we approve of selling flesh for cash. If you're on a stay of leave, you have no right to tell us what to do or not to do."

"Marshal Wilson, aren't you going to do something?" the captain asked, clearly angry—his face was getting redder by the minute. He wasn't used to men talking back to him.

"Like you said, Captain, I'm just here to make the apprehension of the men on the wanted posters all legal and to assist you with the outlaws if the need arises."

"Well, the need arises right now," Captain Holmes spat.

"But these men aren't outlaws," Marshal Wilson replied. "None of 'em look like the wanted posters you showed me, and none of 'em look like soldiers. What do you want me to do? I can't make 'em tell you what they don't know. Ain't that obvious?"

"How about I pay the big fella there to scout for us?" the captain said. "As I'm on leave, I don't have my Indian scouts, so I could use somebody to show me the way. I'll pay you a hundred dollars when we find and apprehend them."

"That's a lot of money to chase down a couple of privates," Levi replied, smiling, but it didn't reach his eyes. "How big of a bounty are on these two deserters?"

"And how is that business of yours, mister?"

"Levi Johnson's the name. Iffin you want me to track for ya, I want to know all I can about who I'm huntin'. The more information, the better."

"The reward is not of importance," Holmes insisted. "I'm making you a fair offer."

"What's fair depends on how dangerous they are, and usually, the size of the bounty will indicate just that." Levi grinned so wide you could see his wisdom teeth. He continued to play with the arrogant officer.

The mountain men all disliked the captain instantly. For them, the lowest forms of life were slavers, scalp hunters, and bounty hunters. The flesh for cash business was unacceptable for all eight men. If it was the marshal alone, they might have treated him differently. They had seen the two so-called outlaws, and the officer and marshal seemed more like villains than the two privates. They just looked like scared young men who got caught up in a whirlwind of trouble and were waiting to be spat out somewhere along their trail of flight.

Captain Holmes sat astride his horse, frowning as he narrowed his eyes and furrowed his brow. You could see the gears churning behind his eyes.

"A thousand dollars—each," Captain Holmes said. "Two thousand for the pair. We want 'em alive if we can."

"Why, so you can take 'im back to hang anyway?" Rusty growled.

Levi whistled. "That's a heck of a lot of money, Captain. I figure they must be just about as dangerous as they get. I'm afraid I'm gonna have to bow out. If they're that dangerous, I could get killed."

"I'll pay you in advance," Captain Holmes said. "All you have to do is find them before they get away."

"Dead men can't spend money," Levi replied and shrugged his shoulders.

"So, that's how it is, hey?" the captain said. "I'll pay any one of you two hundred dollars to hunt these deserters down."

"Why did they desert?" Rusty asked.

"Because they shot and killed their superior officer," Holmes said, now beyond himself.

"That is serious. I wonder why they shot 'im?" Rusty asked. He held his chin in his hand like he was pondering on what the captain said.

"Because they were disobeying orders," the captain said, utterly frustrated. "In times of war, we shoot cowards."

"So, they were kind of defending themselves," Levi said. "How did that work out for 'em?"

"The more I hear about this story, the more I'm drawn to hear more," Rusty said. "What were these orders they were accused of disobeying, if you don't mind me askin'? Don't mind the boys. They ain't all that used to strangers visiting uninvited."

"If you must know, they were ordered to kill savages," Captain Holmes said. "They are no more than cowards for not following orders."

The men on the porch thought back on what the deserters had said. They were ordered to shoot the elderly along with women and children. If that was what they were going to be shot for, not a mountain man one was going to help these representatives of civilized law.

"Well, I sure do hope you get lucky findin' 'im, Captain," Rusty Steel said. "I'm afraid it's too late in the season for us to go traipsing around the mountains. We've got work to do and beaver to trap. But you go on ahead with our blessing. Watch out for that big Crow Indian camp a half day's ride north. You best swing around, or you may find you'll need that invisible army of yours. They don't take kindly to soldiers after y'all killed so many of 'em. Especially with you bein' on your own and all. I doubt they've even seen a marshal before."

All the men on the porch chuckled and some even laughed. Everyone but ex-Captain William Forrester. He kept his eyes glued to his moccasins and ignored the strangers. He hadn't even looked their way.

"So what do you have to say, mister?" the captain asked. "You with the blond hair, blue eyes and empty sleeve."

Forrester acted like he didn't hear him. He turned his head and stared off into space. Unfortunately, this made the officer even more curious.

"Is your friend deaf?" Holmes asked.

"He ain't much of a talker," Angus dryly replied. "Especially with strangers—he's a tad shy, is all."

"You wouldn't know about a pair of deserters, would you there, blondie?" Captain Holmes asked.

The captain eyed the corral and saw only seven horses and eight mules for the eight men on the porch. Holmes didn't make captain because he was stupid—quite the contrary. He was as smart as a whip; now, his mind had turned toward Forrester, and things didn't add up.

Holmes stared at Forrester for a full minute, then he huffed, unhooked his cover from his pistol grip, and slipped his cavalry hat on his head. He nodded, wheeled his horse around, and headed for the open gate. When he got to the trail, he stopped his horse for a moment and shot his gaze over his shoulder at Will Forrester. Finally, their eyes locked. The mountain man's showed open aggression. There was no fear there at all like he'd expected. This man wasn't shy like they said. Why had they lied? He obviously had a secret he didn't want known. Why else would he respond this way in the presence of an Army officer?

Maybe on the way back down with the two prisoners, he would stop and investigate some more. Maybe there was more there than met the eye. He was sure the blond-haired mountain man was hiding something from him—an Army officer. Why could that be, he wondered?

The captain nudged his horse's flanks and rode up the trail behind the deserters. In a couple of minutes, all that was left of the riders was a cloud of dust.

"Whatcha reckon, Will?" Levi asked. "Is this fella gonna be a problem?"

"He gives me a bad feeling," Forrester replied. "I could see it in his eyes; he knows I'm hiding something."

"Whatcha hidin', pilgrim?" Rusty asked. "You've got nothin' to hide from, son, and I was there with you boys when you saw the worst of what this country has to throw at cha. You gave it all you've got, so you shouldn't feel guilty about a darned thing."

"You go tell Captain Holmes that," Forrester said. "I doubt we've seen the last of him."

"Oh, I can guarantee ya that." Rusty chuckled. "We're gonna dog these strangers and see what they be up to on our mountain. They think they're the law, but we're the law here. Maybe we'll give 'em a little surprise."

THE CAPTAIN

"I DON'T LIKE THE LOOKS OF THAT BUNCH OF GRIZZLY bears," Captain Holmes said. "Especially that big young fellow with the smart aleck mouth. I think he was teasing me, trying to lead me on to get information. How dare he speak to a captain of the United States Army in such a manner. I saw all those rifles and pistols too. They had to have known we were coming. They were shy one horse too. I counted eight mules and seven horses. I'd say that bunch is up to no good. I wouldn't be surprised if they weren't all outlaws living up here to evade a noose. Anybody could change their names and live here, where past crimes wouldn't be resolved."

The marshal noticed the mention of changed names and felt a nagging sensation. It was his conscience. He, too, had been another man. What would Captain Holmes do if he knew Wilson's past? He wondered what he had gotten himself into. The five hundred dollars wouldn't do him much good if he was dead. Still, it was more money than he had ever imagined. He could buy himself a piece of land, start a ranch, and give up the life he'd chosen to replace the last one.

"I saw you lookin' funny at the shy fella," Marshal Wilson said as he eyed the captain. "You got the strangest look on your face. It was almost like you knew him."

"There's something about him that I couldn't put my finger on," the captain replied. "It was almost like I saw a young me in him—but somehow different. No, I've never met the man before, but I've met somebody that reminds me of him. At least, I think I have. It'll come to me directly. My mind is like a steel trap. It just takes some coaxing to bring some memories from the past. Things come to me like that."

"Don't you think you've got enough on your plate without gettin' distracted by something you guess is suspicious?" Marshal Wilson asked. "I'm not interested in nothin' more than the two deserters. Remember, like we agreed? If you wanna go on some wild goose chase, you'll have to go it alone. I'm going to see to it the arrest is all legal, and if you decide to do something else, I'll wait for you down the mountain. I have no intention of getting stuck up here snowed in."

"Look at that sky," Holmes said. "There's not a sign of snow, and it's as warm as toast during the day. You're making a mountain out of an anthill."

"And it's just reaching freezing of an evening. Every night we have to keep a bigger fire going to stay warm," Marshal Wilson grumbled. "Lucky thing I brought my heavy coat. I'm not partial to snow or freezing temperatures. It makes my bones ache."

"You don't need to exaggerate," Captain Holmes

said. "You'll get well paid for your services, so you can't complain."

"Yeah, and of a morning, the mud puddles are frozen like the grass. Everything is coated in frost first thing. Soon it'll snow, and it will be too late to make it back down. Have you seen any shelter anywhere besides the mountain men you impressed with your wit and charm?"

The captain bumped his horse down, spur to spur with Marshal Wilson as he casually pulled his glove tight and unexpectedly backhanded the marshal so hard it knocked him off his horse. He sat up in the dirt, dazed and confused, as he shook his head to clear his mind. It took him a few seconds to work out what had happened. When he looked up and locked eyes with the officer, his blood turned to ice. The look in the captain's eyes would peel paint off a wall. His mouth was no more than a gash, and he had his hand wrapped around his pistol's grip.

The marshal's first instinct was to shoot the man, just like the bully back in the bar in Illinois. But he knew he wouldn't be fast enough. Not with the captain's hand on his revolver. It was like he was taunting him on purpose, but Marshal Wilson wasn't a fool either. He'd bide his time until after they found the outlaws. Maybe he wouldn't take the prisoners back down with the captain. It would be better if he took them without the arrogant officer. Nobody knew where he was anyway. If he disappeared, Wilson doubted he would be missed.

"Remember who you work for," Captain Holmes growled. His eyes were full of anger; the marshal saw it and kept his mouth shut. He didn't want to get shot. There was danger in the lawman's eyes too, but Holmes didn't see it. He was too self-centered to look at another man as an equal. He felt he was superior.

That was one of the reasons he so enjoyed killing Indians. Even if they were old, women and children. He enjoyed them the most. He knew that with their demise, the genocide would continue as planned. Dead women didn't reproduce, and dead boys didn't grow up to be warriors. He was just balancing things out for the years to come, and for the great civilization machine to arrive this far west.

Marshal Wilson suddenly realized he had side-kicked up with a lunatic. He'd thought the whole trip was a bit crazy this time of year, but Holmes had offered him five hundred dollars of the bounties. If he ever could, it would take him years to save that much money. Now, he began to wonder about the man he'd hired on with. He hadn't thought about it at first. He was a captain in the US Army, after all.

He wondered who he was riding with and if he would end up just another dead body left beside the trail. Or would it be the captain that died? He doubted both men would ride back down the mountains. Would the captain kill a man over five hundred dollars in gold coins? He figured it could go either way at the moment, but he knew he had to watch out once they found the bounties.

He would have to sleep with one eye open, fearing Holmes might slit his throat during the night. There would only be two outlaws as witnesses, so he knew the captain could get away with it. The marshal believed Holmes would know it too. The situation could go either way now that the cards were on the table face up.

He wiggled his jaw with his hand and stood,

brushing off the dust with his hat. Without a word, he climbed astride his horse. Blood trickled from the corner of his mouth—he wiped it off with the back of his hand. His tongue fished around in his mouth and he spat out a tooth. He kept his eyes pointed up the trail as he led the way. He didn't like having the captain behind him, but they were more likely to find the outlaws with him tracking. Most officers weren't much at the complicated details of living rough.

The marshal was slightly better at tracking than the captain, but they didn't have to be geniuses. The fleeing privates did not attempt to hide their tracks. Their only thought was escape. Wilson was beginning to believe these soldiers weren't all that bad and perhaps the captain was the dangerous one. It was beginning to sound like some drummed-up charges and exaggerated bounties for unknown criminals. Maybe it was a scheme to make two thousand dollars. It was a fortune for most of the population, including field officers like Captain Holmes, and for Marshal Jack Wilson too.

The Kansas marshal began to believe the entire thing may have been created by the same man who sought justice. Who was the outlaw here? Things were beginning to get fuzzy as they moved into the gray area of the law. Of course, Jack had left his home in Illinois. He killed a man in a barroom fight and had to run himself. He landed in Kansas and offered his hand as a marshal. He was good with his gun and no longer used his real name, Joe Wicks. It had been that simple. Of course, he wasn't wanted in Kansas, but he knew he, too, lived a lie. He wondered if the captain had something to hide, too, or was he as squeaky clean as he claimed. The marshal doubted it.

As they rode higher, they had to walk the horses more as their footing faltered. The ice from the morning dew had melted and turned to slippery mud. Both men's boots were covered in mud, and as they trudged forward, the wet earth sucked at their boots. A gunshot sounded off in the distance. Both men slipped their rifles from their shoulders and lay them across their laps. They exchanged glances, and the captain took the lead. It had to be Privates Zillow and Jones. Who else would be crazy enough to be up here?

The captain thought back to the eight men that lived in the compound. He wondered what had brought them here and how long they had lived like the heathens. Still, the blue-eyed, blond mountain man didn't seem to fit with the rest. There was something about him that was civilized, just like Holmes. It was like he came from the same thread as him but was in different clothing.

"Follow me, and we'll catch these two once and for all," Captain Holmes said.

"Whatcha think they were shootin' at?" the marshal asked. "Maybe there's a bunch of Indians out yonder."

"You worry too much for a marshal," Holmes observed. "It's obvious you were never in the Army." It was meant as an insult.

"I serve in my way," Wilson retorted. "I keep the peace and have more jurisdiction over this land than you do."

"Not when it regards soldiers," Holmes spat.

"A civilian judge made out the bounty, so I'm the one that's gonna present the warrant," Marshal Wilson growled.

If he sucker-punches me again, I'm gonna kill 'im, the US Marshal thought.

Privates Todd Zillow and Jimmy Jones continued to press their horses. As they climbed higher, the trails got steeper and more difficult for the horses to navigate. The frost from the night before had melted, making it muddy and slippery. They had to walk them by the lead to keep them from falling off the trail and down a two-hundred-foot cliff. The animals huffed and groaned, forced to go much harder than was wise. It came as no surprise when Jimmy's horse slipped and fell to the bottom.

It seemed like it happened in slow motion. They were walking along, and the private saw the horse's hooves slip and slide, then its back legs lost traction and slipped to the side. Jimmy felt the reins tug then slip away. This sent the animal banging against the canyon wall to the bottom. They heard a dull thud when it landed.

When it hit the ground below, it must have broken its back because it lay there squealing and moaning. It looked like it was going to die a slow death. Jimmy shook his head, and before Todd could stop him, he took the shot to put him out of his pain and misery. The sounds from below were instantly silenced, but the gunshot's echo bounced across the mountains a half dozen times.

"Now you've gone and done it," Todd spat. "They'll know which way to chase us now that you've announced where we are."

"I'm sorry, but I just couldn't watch it suffer like that," Jimmy said. "You know as well as I do that they'll have no problem following us. We're all on the same trail."

"Next, it'll be us getting shot," Todd growled. "Now, what are we gonna do?"

"What we don't wanna do is panic," Jimmy said. "That animal saved my bacon a time or two, so I had to do what was right. Maybe I'll get a chance to shoot Captain Holmes before he shoots us first."

The two frightened men didn't know what to do now. Against all they learned, they rode double on Todd's horse. They knew it wouldn't last. As expected, the animal keeled over three hours later and dropped dead in its tracks. Lucky for the riders, they were expecting it, so they had just enough time to jump off and not get a leg trapped under the animal. Blood came from its mouth.

"Dagnabit, now what're we gonna do?" Todd asked. "Now the posse followin' us is gonna know exactly where we are. They might not have seen the horse down below, but with one dead on the trail, they can't help but see. There's no way you and me can drag it away on our own."

Jimmy looked up the trail and then into the trees and woods. "Let's take a trail hard enough that the men chasing us will have to abandon their horses too. Lookee over there at that Indian path up the side of that hill. It's way too steep for a horse to climb. That way, we don't have to keep goin' up where it's getting' mighty cold at night. Maybe we can go down the other side."

Todd looked at his partner and said, "Why, that sounds like a grand idea. I doubt the captain chasing us will like walking, and the marshal won't wanna lose his horse. If they did leave their horses behind, they'd be afoot in a few hours. I've seen signs of Indians for the last day. I doubt they would hesitate to take two horses, and I don't believe they know the difference between the captain and us, although they may know what a marshal is."

"Stop talkin', and let's skinny up that steep trail," Jimmy said.

They ran for the other side of the trail and across a crop of rocks before they got to the footpath over the next ridge. They didn't know what was behind it. They were worried about what was behind them, not what was in front of them. They knew the law would be biting at their heels soon. They were running out of time, and they didn't expect less than a firing squad or noose if they got caught, so they had nothing to lose at that point.

The trail became so steep they had to grab roots and plants to pull themselves up toward the top. It was obvious the trail was hardly used.

"I doubt Indians climb this dad-gummed trail," Jimmy said. "It looks more like it's for goats than human beings."

Both men huffed and stopped every ten or twenty yards to catch their breath. It didn't look so steep from a distance, but now they were nearing a vertical climb. As they clawed their way up, they knew they would never be able to climb back down the same way again. They stopped to breathe at a small flat landing halfway to the top. Both men gobbled up the air as they struggled for oxygen. Jimmy looked on the other side of the valley, where the dead horse lay.

"No sign of the captain and the marshal yet," Jimmy said as his brow furrowed. "If we can get to the top before they show, maybe they'll think we kept following the same trail."

"I doubt that works because there won't be any boot prints farther up the trail," Todd said. "It might slow 'em down a little, but they'll figure we've taken another path soon enough."

"If we're in sight, he might take a couple of shots at us," Jimmy said as he stood and began to claw his way up the trail again. "Be careful where you step, or you'll slide right back down."

Todd shot another glance over his shoulder to see if there was any sign of Captain Holmes. He didn't see anything, but he knew he was coming. He could feel it in his guts. The captain was right behind them. Perspiration shined on their faces, and their shirts stuck to their backs as rivulets of sweat ran down the small of their backs.

CROW INDIANS

THERE WAS HARDLY A THING THAT HAPPENED IN THIS PART of the Rocky Mountains that War Chief Hachta didn't know about, and the Army soldiers were no exception. He had been watching the first two from a distance when one of their horses fell down a gorge. Their big, tall horses weren't made for this rugged terrain like the Indian ponies were. He had another seven warrior braves spying on the bluecoat that chased them.

They knew very well what soldiers looked like. They were the men promoting the slaughter of their tribe and their food every chance they got. It was the same with the Sioux and Blackfeet. There was a marshal with him. Just because he wore a badge didn't make him special in the Rocky Mountains, though.

Anybody could pin a badge on. It didn't give them the right to trespass on Indian territory. White men had to request permission to come into their mountains and plains. The eight mountain men who lived a half day's ride from the Crow camp had humbly asked to stay and never caused the Crow problems. Sometimes they even helped the tribe. The newcomers weren't humble enough to know this land wasn't theirs to travel. Even the mountain men imagined that one day they, too, would be asked to leave.

They followed the White men without being seen. With these, it wasn't all that difficult to do. They obviously weren't experienced mountain men. The marshal looked like a city lawman. The war chief was curious why a soldier and a marshal were chasing two more soldiers. Then again, White men were always doing strange things.

They were dangerously close to discovering their camp. If they happened to find it, they might have to die. Otherwise, Washington would send more soldiers once they knew where to locate them. It would be kill them or move the entire camp. Hachta didn't think his tribe's new chief would be prepared to move a hundred teepees to save the trespassers' lives.

Chief Chato would immediately order his men to bring the White men to him, and they would be tortured and put to death unless they had a good reason and even a better story to steer the minds of the Crow Indians in a different direction.

Of course, Hachta had seen other soldiers when he rode to the valley below. Some were said to have come to the Rendezvous to buy stock and horses if there was a patrol in the area. Most of them were found on the plains where it was easy to spot the enemy. They seldom strayed into the mountains—especially this time of year when winter was just around the corner.

The soldier and marshal that were chasing them

must have wanted them awfully bad to take such a chance on the local Indian tribes and the unpredictable weather of the Rockies. Hachta wondered if they had something of value or was it as simple as revenge. It might even be for money. That was what motivated the White man the most—that and land, which appeared to be their main obsession.

When the second horse died, it was no surprise to the Indians either. They thought the horse being ridden double should have died long before it did. Now, the fools were climbing up a trail they shouldn't be. He wondered if the men chasing them would arrive in time to see where they were going. If they did, the situation could become serious.

"Let's go hide beside the trail, so maybe we can hear what they are saying," Hachta said to his warriors. "I know the White man's tongue. It may help to know who they are before we capture or kill them. Maybe they will be brave and fight and die like warriors, or maybe they will cower. At least the first two. Fear is chiseled on their faces already."

The war party kept a close eye on the two men fleeing, but they kept a closer eye on the Army captain. Maybe the men they chased could be on the Indians' side. Why would a White Army chief be chasing two lowly Army braves? That was the question that Hachta wanted answered. Above all, he was a patient man and knew it was his best virtue. Soon, he would discover what they were doing there.

He sat and watched as the folly played out. He saw the two men fleeing disappear up at the end of the trail. He chuckled because he was aware of what would happen next. The Crow war chief knew every tree, rock, and hiding place within twenty miles of their camp. It was his responsibility to make sure everyone remained safe.

He was surprised when the White Army chief and the lawman abandoned their horses. He chuckled again when they hobbled them like that would keep them from disappearing. He shot an arrow into the sky, signaling the men on the other side to take their animals. It wasn't stealing for the Crow because the White men left their animals to their fates on their land. Anyone abandoning a horse on the plains or in the wilderness should be ready to have it vanish.

He was even more surprised when the two middle-aged men with graying hair followed the two young soldiers. There seemed no limit to their stupidity. Didn't they know that several Indian tribes lived in these mountains and the valleys below? They had been stumbling all over their mountain and weren't even aware they were being watched the whole time.

Black and blond scalps hung from the war chief's belt. He was the only one to wear a brace of pistols. A bow was strapped across his back with a quiver of arrows. His long shirt fell to his knees. He wore a loincloth above his knee-high moccasins. His face appeared chiseled in stone, and he was emotionless as he continued to stare at the folly below. His hair was so black that it almost had a blue tint and fell below his shoulders. He watched as the marshal and the captain closed in on the soldiers.

Hachta stood and nodded, and he and his braves raced for the camp. They had to inform Chief Chato that visitors' arrival would be imminent. He knew how

Army officers treated Indians, so he didn't ignore the threat these trespassers posed. All soldiers were considered dangerous, and the Indians all over the Rocky Mountains knew they had killed entire tribes for no reason. They appeared to be hell-bent on radicalizing the few that remained after they finished their massacre.

A few minutes later, Hachta and his chief stood before the tribe as the other braves shooed the women, children, and elderly into their teepees. They didn't know what to expect from the soldiers. They had heard these men kill more than warrior braves. Soon, they were painting their faces to make them appear even more fierce than they already were.

They were waiting on the privates first. Then would come the Army chief and the lawman with the tin star on his chest. Nobody moved an inch as they waited for the intruders. They could already smell White man's soap and knew they would be clawing up the other side of the cliff before them.

Hachta had been in the camp waiting. He had informed Chief Chato of the trespassers, and he was ordered to assemble the warrior braves. The women were hiding in the teepees with the elders and the children. The Indian gossip had made it to the Crow camp, and they had heard everything about the captain who killed women and children. He even slaughtered the aging for what he called his cause. He actively participated in the genocide the Army perpetrated on the Native Indian population.

The Crow camp stretched from canyon wall to canyon wall. The way in was vast and wide, but the way out the back was narrow and treacherous. A hundred teepees were scattered as numerous fires sent black smoke skyward. No women or children were to be seen. Everything looked like it had been dropped, and the people vanished. Only the warriors stood behind the tribal Chief Chato and War Chief Hachta.

The braves had even had the time to paint their faces for when they finally faced the trespassers. Streaks of red, green, and white made strikingly ferocious war masks. Some wore headdresses of fur or horns; all of them were armed with lances, bows, and arrows, and some even had rifles. The chief had a Tennessee long rifle cradled in his arms.

The crowd of men wasn't nervous or excited. They sat around fires on logs while they awaited orders from their chief. He was deep in conversation with Hachta.

"What do you wish me to do with the soldiers?" Hachta asked. "The soldier with the marshal is the chief with the reputation of killing women and children. The men fleeing from them are still a mystery to me. It must be some White man's crazy notion of coming to the mountains just before the first snows. They don't know how heavy they come and how deep the snow gets. They could be snowed in for weeks or perish from the cold."

"We will see that they won't have time to suffer such consequences," Chief Chato said ominously. "Capture them, and we will give them a trial here in camp. Then we will decide how to deal with them. Maybe they have a noble reason for trespassing. We won't condemn them until they speak. Then if they are guilty, as you say, you and your men can have them. I have no use for such people. Nature is hard enough to live with, let alone more White people. We must keep enough of them here to trade for the things we need and can't buy. Rusty Steel is a good man and isn't like these soldiers—at least not the captain. The others have yet to be heard. Then they will be tested."

The men assembled and stared at the side of the stronghold and waited. They all knew it was just a matter of time. Indians were more patient than White men, so they stood or sat as still as stones in the blazing sun without so much as blinking an eye. Each one desired to show he was more noble and fierce than the others.

When the first two soldiers came tumbling down the hill too steep to climb, they rolled to the edge of the camp before they could stop. When they fell, it happened so suddenly they didn't even get a glimpse at the Crow camp until they were sitting at the bottom. The blood drained from the soldiers' faces, and their eyes spread wide as fear grasped their souls. The last place a US Army soldier wanted to be was in the middle of a large Indian camp in the middle of the wilderness.

The warriors roared, laughing at the puzzled faces of the two White men sitting in the dirt. The men's eyes flashed back to the top, and as expected, the captain and the marshal came in minutes, just like the privates. They rolled down, trying without success to stop their fall, finally coming to a halt at the warriors' feet.

Captain Holmes gasped for air. He went for his pistols, but they had fallen out of his belt on the tumble down. His rifle was strapped to his back, but if he made a move for it, he believed he would die instantly. Over fifty armed warriors stood before him, and their eyes shot daggers at the officer.

For the most part, the Crow Indians initially ignored

the privates and the marshal. They sat in the dirt, afraid to move a muscle or say a word in case they were noticed. They didn't want to bring any attention to themselves. They averted their eyes and tried as hard as possible to shrink in size and disappear.

In the distance, they heard laughter bouncing off the canyon walls. Hachta smiled when he heard his friend Rusty Steel laughing up at the guard post. He put his fingers to his lips and whistled three long blasts. The mountain men stood on the boulder high above in the distance and waved their rifles. Then they turned and disappeared down the back of the large rock formation.

Fifteen minutes later, Rusty Steel led Levi and Forrester into the camp. Every warrior was present and hostile-looking. Rusty laughed like he thought such a show of force funny. He was a mystery for the new young mountain men, and they often were confused by his actions.

When the warrior braves saw how proud and unafraid Rusty entered their stronghold, they looked at him, and their eyes turned friendly. They knew who he was, but every man was tested constantly to see if he had the grit to be a warrior. Steel was believed by the Crow to be a White warrior. He had lived many years with the Indians and knew more about their ways than any White man they had ever known.

The faces on the first two were comical. They tumbled down out of control without even enough time to see they were falling into a large Crow camp. It wasn't until they hit the bottom that they saw what they had dropped into. They blinked in confusion as their faces expressed their puzzlement.

All Chief Chato had to do was nod his head, and

without a word, four warriors grabbed the men and disarmed them. They didn't even struggle; they were so shocked to find where they were: right in front of more hostile Indians than they had ever seen in their life.

Minutes behind them came the marshal first, and soon after him, Captain Holmes tumbled down to the bottom of the hill. Every wrinkle on his face was caked in dust, but the fury of anger still showed on his face. He spat the dirt from his mouth. He turned his angry eyes on the two men who appeared in charge. Despite the situation, he wore a snarl on his lips and daggers in his eyes. Maybe he hadn't yet realized how much trouble he was already in.

Hachta put his fingers to his mouth and whistled three sharp blasts to signal to Rusty that he could come down. He immediately saw his White friends waving their rifles in the air. They turned and ran down the back of the boulder.

The war chief signaled his warriors with a flip of his hand, and they grabbed the captain and the marshal. These two weren't so passive about being manhandled by the warrior braves. These men required four each to subdue them. The marshal didn't stop swearing and spitting at his captors the whole time.

Now, the captain suddenly realized where he was and became confused. A moment ago, he was just about to apprehend his deserters; everything instantly changed once they reached the top of the trail. They had dropped over the other side and into the lion's mouth. Sixty pairs of angry eyes stared at them.

The Crow Indians didn't blink an eye. The marshal's face said it all. He had seen where he was and had already surrendered to what was to come. He, too, was puzzled about how he got to where he was when they had been minutes from apprehending the outlaws.

Now, they were in the hands of the enemy. The soldiers didn't even know what tribe they were, although they had been warned that a large Crow camp was up here somewhere. They had just found it.

LEVI, WILL, & RUSTY

"WHATCHA THINK ABOUT ALL THIS OUTLAW BUSINESS?" Rusty asked. "I don't know which ones I like least, the supposed villains or the posse of two. How dangerous can a man be if only two men are huntin' 'em?"

"It all depends how ornery the pair doing the chasing are," Forrester said. "One carries a badge, but that doesn't mean he's honest. I believe those two are bounty hunters. Before he pinned that badge on his chest, he could have been pretty much anyone."

"I figure 'em for hired guns although they're polite enough," Levi replied, "but I still got a bad feelin' about 'em."

"They're offering us handsome money to track for them," Forrester said. "Whatever they were before, they're lawmen now. You saw the badge. I believe that counts for something."

"Up here, the only things that count are your word and your stones, son," Rusty said, "and ya don't wanna break either one for nobody."

They roped the horses in the corral. Forrester

saddled Angus's gray and Levi's Tac. They decided it would be better to leave the white stallion in the stables, especially as it had a US Army brand on its left hip. Will had never thought his horse would bring him trouble, but for all appearances, it looked like he stole the animal. If the captain found it, Will would be forced to fess up to everything and take his chances.

He still felt enough military running through his veins to feel intimidated. He had always had officers and peers above him, and he'd always tried to do his best to please them. But why did he feel the same about the captain trespassing on their mountain? He couldn't answer the question, but just the same, he was intimidated even though they both held the same rank.

"Maybe we shouldn't be takin' any horses," Levi said. "With the state of their mounts, I doubt they make it to the end of the day. The same goes for the captain and the marshal. All four of them have run their animals to death. Maybe we'd fare better if we went on foot. It would make it much more difficult for them to see us."

"By golly, you're right," Rusty said. "Them boys won't be riding much longer because there's no way those horses are gonna hold up at that pace. Why, even my mule struggles once you get farther up the trail a few hours. We also know this forest like the back of our hands, so we can take shortcuts and wait for them farther up the trail. Grab your guns, boys, before we run out of light. We might be able to catch up with them long before we lose the sun."

In five minutes, they grabbed the sacks of provisions Angus had prepared for them. They each strapped a rifle over their shoulders and shoved several pistols into their belts. The more bullets they had if things went south, the better chances they had to survive. They didn't know much about the two privates, but the marshal and captain had killed before and wouldn't hesitate to act again if the call came. Of that, they had no doubt.

"You do know any sane man would walk away from this and not stick their noses in where they don't belong," Levi said.

"I wanna know where they're going and what they're really up to," Forrester said. "Whether I like it or not, I'm still tied to the Army—in a way, for life. That was my entire education. Except for what I've learned here, of course."

"I thought the Army went with the arm." Rusty chuckled. "I believe losin' that arm might have been the best thing that's happened to ya. I've noticed the change in ya from when we first met until now, and I'd say you aren't even the same man. Why, you're more of a man without the arm."

"I have to agree with Rusty," Levi said. "Even I like ya more now." They all laughed as they vanished into the forest.

One moment they were there, and the next, they weren't. Like Indians, they shadow shifted instinctively, making themselves difficult to see, and at the same time, leaving hardly any track. Even Forrester was a pathfinder now, and Levi was as good as Rusty. He learned about the wilderness with the hunger of a rabid dog.

They raced through the woods, knowing the place of every stone on the trail, every waterhole and hiding spot to be found. They knew what direction the two parties of men were going in. Still, they knew that when traveling through the forest especially fast, you had to be extra careful and use all your senses to know what was ahead of you. Rusty led the way as branches slapped their faces and arms. Bloody scratches from thorns tattooed their cheeks.

Now, even Forrester ran silently through the forest since he traded his boots for an old pair of moccasins he found in the cabin. Rusty didn't even remember who they belonged to, but they fit him like a glove.

"I wonder if that big pack of wolves is still runnin' about out here," Forrester whispered as they stopped for a moment to listen for any out-of-place sounds and smell for revealing scents. "I'd hate to run into their teeth instead of the soldiers."

"They won't attack three armed men, but if they catch ya alone, they might have a go," Rusty said. "Hush now. I smell sweat, so we're gettin' close."

"But ain't the Crow camp just over that rise?" Levi whispered.

"That's why I said shush," Rusty retorted.

They dropped to their bellies and crawled to the top of the ridge. There was a giant boulder at the end which they could climb. If they were careful, they should have a picture window view of the valley and the Crow camp below. This was where Crow warriors stood guard in times of war. Now, Rusty used it to spy on the soldiers, the marshal, and his friends, the Crow.

They noticed a motion to their left when they reached the boulder's edge. They saw the two privates clawing their way up the ridge. Levi pulled out his spyglass and had a look down the trail behind them. Not fifteen minutes away, he could see a dust cloud rising from the treetops.

"That'll be the captain and the marshal ridin'
behind the two fleeing for their lives," Levi said, amazed
at what he was watching unfold. "They're just about to
step out of the fire and right into the skillet."

Rusty couldn't help but chuckle at the humor in it
all. He liked to fancy himself as a master of strange
behavior in human beings. It was something that fasci-
nated him, and so it took him a while to stop snickering.
Levi didn't see anything funny about what was about to
happen. Forrester just looked on in horror. They were
all heading for the last place they wanted to be.

Levi watched as the two privates arrived at the top,
which was an illusion as there was no flat spot to gain
their footing after such a steep climb. They could never
climb back down anyway. It was so steep down the
other side that they found themselves tumbling down
the hill, sliding and rolling over and over until they hit
bottom. Dozens of pairs of eyes stared at them.

Levi huffed as he swept the spyglass across the
mountain to the trail behind them. He saw a dead horse
lying in the middle of the trail. The captain and the
marshal were inspecting the animal. The officer was
fingering the US Army brand with his fingers. The
marshal instantly saw where the tracks stopped, went to
the right, and then disappeared over the rocks. But he
could see the rugged trail they took from all the roots
and plants they uprooted on their way up. They had to
struggle to get up the hill.

A wolf howled somewhere—it wasn't that far away.
It made everybody stop for a second, ensuring the pack
wasn't near them. Everybody in the forest feared large
packs of ravenous wolves, and this was the most significant pack ever heard to roam the Rockies. This one

numbered over twenty and was growing, when wolf packs usually ran from five to nine members with the odd pack of fifteen.

But nobody had ever seen a pack of twenty man-eaters like those currently running wild across this part of the Rockies. The mountain men had thought about hunting them, but they saw it was too dangerous. They could turn on them despite the rifles and pistols if they got them cornered. There were too many to kill them all. As soon as they shot one or two, they vanished. There were so many of them they became bold and brave in front of men and animals alike. They only avoided the grizzly bear, but even they didn't scare them as they could easily outrun them.

Levi saw vultures circling above the marshal and captain, but he saw another dozen circling above a spot farther down the trail. That was when he saw the horse that had fallen off the cliff.

"They've lost both their horses," Levi said. "I wonder what the captain is gonna do now. I doubt the marshal will take kindly to leavin' his horse abandoned for a passing Indian to take for his own."

"Indians believe if someone don't care enough to keep their animals safe, it's fair game to take 'im," Rusty said. "See how not taking our horses worked out for us? Takin' an abandoned horse in the wilderness ain't even considered a hangin' offense."

"I'd like you to convey that to the captain," Forrester whispered. "If he sees the US Army brand on my stallion, I feel he will think differently."

To the mountain men's surprise, the captain and even the marshal hobbled their horses and left them to graze. They crossed the rock outcrop and started to climb the same hill the privates had just scaled. They weren't as young as the two deserters, and the climb proved to be more difficult for them. The marshal did reasonably well, but the captain slipped and slid back down three times. His fancy riding boots weren't built for such rough terrain. Levi watched him through his spyglass; even from a distance, you could see his face was as red as a tomato. His princely uniform soon became covered in dirt, as did his face.

Levi passed the spyglass to his friend Will, and when he looked, he couldn't help but smile.

"The captain looks a little worse for wear." Forrester snickered with his hand over his mouth.

"Look at that," Rusty said as he pointed to the hobbled horses.

They weren't even out of sight, and the Crow Indians were already running off with their horses. The captain and marshal were so focused on climbing what was nearly a cliff they didn't even notice when their animals vanished in a puff of dust, much like a magic act. Rusty stifled another laugh.

"Now they've lost their horses too." Rusty grinned. "But they won't be needin' them where they're goin'. That captain ain't nearly as smart as he thinks he is. He's makin' every mistake in the book. Now he's gonna see just how stupid he is."

"Shouldn't we do something?" Forrester asked, shocked. "We can't let them kill an Army captain. It may bring more soldiers up here."

"Now you're talkin' foolish, son." Rusty smiled. "Do you really think anybody knows where these two fools are? Most bounty hunters I know are tight-lipped about what they say concerning their bounty. They'd have every man in the country who's willin' to trade flesh for money after those two iffin they knew how much they were worth."

"How much is a man's life worth?" Forrester asked in a hushed voice, like he was afraid to hear the answer.

"I reckon that all depends on who's evaluatin' 'im," Rusty said. "Iffin they be outlaws like these two, the price is clear, although I never like to put a man's worth in dollars. Most men are worth more than just money."

"Who do you think is worth more?" Levi asked. "The men being chased or the men chasin' 'em?"

"If first appearances mean anything, I'd go with the privates," Rusty replied. "Most Kansas marshals come from someplace they've run away from. A captain up here has to be up to no good. The Army made a pact with Washington to rid the country of Indians and buffalo. So far, they're doin' a hell of a job of it."

"But you were a captain, Will, and you're up here with us," Levi said. "I reckon it all depends on which twister sweeps ya up and away and where it spits you out."

As they lay on the large boulder warmed from the sun, they watched until the captain and the marshal, too, disappeared over the cliff. A puff of dust rose with the wind.

They heard three shrill whistles. "That'll be Hachta tellin' us it's all clear to visit the village. They must have all four White men. Let's go see what they plan to do with 'em."

THE STRONGHOLD

HACHTA WAS STANDING BESIDE CHIEF CHATO WHEN THEY arrived. Rusty knew the chief before when he was a warrior brave. He was the son-in-law of the old chief. Politics were the same everywhere. Hachta had thought he would be selected to be the next leader, but it wasn't meant to be. This chief wasn't old and would live a long life, depriving Hachta of ever becoming the head of his people. He'd dreamed of this, but he was mature enough to know life often didn't give men what they wanted. It gave whatever Mother Nature, and the wicked men of the world, threw at them.

The four White men sat in a row with their backs to the canyon wall. Their hands were tied behind their backs, and two old women were poking them with sticks. Minor cuts and bruises covered their faces. The captain's uniform was dirty and tattered. The warrior braves hadn't been gentle, but the true torturers were the widows and old maids of the tribe. They were often used to inflict pain on the Indians' enemies. They were full of hate and vengeance, and they took their time because no one awaited them in their teepees. All they had was disdain for White men and, in most cases, their long, lonely lives. This respite of administering pain and suffering somehow made them special despite their loneliness.

When Rusty led Levi and Forrester into the Indian camp, Hachta greeted him like one of the tribe. They had helped feed the Indians many times and fought to protect the mountains from trespassers, just like the Crow Indians.

"It's good to see you, Rusty," Hachta said, smiling. "I see you haven't thrown the two young mountain men out of your cabin yet. You must be getting old."

"We're the same age, partner." Rusty laughed. "So ya best not go there. I see you found these four trespassers. What have they had to say for themselves?"

"As we speak, they are finding out I speak English," Hachta said. "Sometimes it is good not to tell strangers our secrets until we have time to listen. The soldier with the fancy hat and pretty strings on his shoulders is the Army war chief—the others call him Captain Holmes. The marshal is with him. The men fleeing called him Marshal Wilson from Kansas. They are chasing the other two, but we don't know why yet. Chief Chato wants to have an Indian trail. This will bring him a lot of attention. Capturing an Army chief will make him famous—this Captain Holmes is known among White men as an Indian fighter. He is known among the Crow as the murderer of old men, women, and children."

"Whatcha mean, captured?" Rusty asked. "These fools rolled right into your camp all on their lonesome. There wasn't anybody captured. Hell, it's more like they surrendered or fell into a trap they made for themselves. I've never seen anything more stupid than the antics of these four."

"Still, there will be a trial to make a lot of noise," Hachta whispered. "This will solidify his position in the tribe. All new chiefs try to make a statement early in their first months or year as leader of the tribe. He is making his move now. I'll never be able to achieve my goal."

"I know you always wanted to be chief," Rusty said under his breath. "They passed the wrong man over. Politics is what that is, just like with White folks."

Chief Chato said something in Crow, and the warriors bound the men's feet and carried them to the community lodge. There were so many warriors they carried them over their heads as they tormented them with terrifying war cries. The sour old maids continued to poke them with sticks. The privates' eyes were spread wide. The marshal's mouth was no more than a gash, like he knew the jig was up, but Captain Holmes continued to try to lash out and spit on his captors. It appeared he still hadn't seen what a dangerous position he was in. Arrogance flashed in his eyes despite being outnumbered overwhelmingly.

When the captain's eyes met those of Rusty Steel, he screamed, "You're an outlaw too! You were with the men I questioned about the deserters. I'll see that you hang for this. And you, too, Mister Blondie. I remember where I saw your face. It was the front of a newspaper about some fancy expedition back in Leavenworth, Kansas. What happened to your command, or did you kill all of them too? None of you know who you're fooling with. If you let me go now, I may consider leniency. If you put things right, I may forgive your oversight, which would leave you in a better negotiating position."

Rusty frowned like he was frightened for a moment, then burst out laughing. The captain's face turned a darker red as a vein pulsated on his forehead.

"I suppose it depends on which place you're standin'." Rusty smiled. "From where I'm standin', everything looks fine for us. From where you're standin', it looks like you won't be seein' anybody hang or kill any more Indian women and children."

"I don't kill women and children," Captain Holmes spat. He was nearly frothing at the mouth.

"Whatcha say, young fellas?" Rusty said to the privates. "Don't worry—the captain's got no say-so up here. He's trespassing on Crow land with intentions of violence and has been accused of genocide in the past. I never even knew the word until Will told me what it meant. Needless to say, I was mighty put out in you, Captain Holmes. And here I thought you were an honorable man."

"You're all mixed up in this. I knew it the first time I laid eyes on you scum," Holmes growled. He was so angry he bit his tongue, and blood dripped from the corner of his mouth. "Every last one of you will pay when I return with my soldiers."

"When you find yourself in a hole much like you find yourself right now, I'd suggest you stop digging, Captain." Levi smiled.

"Here in a spell, the chief is gonna hold you on trial before all the tribe's elders, chiefs, and medicine men." Rusty grinned. "You're gonna get tried for killin' women and children. That and old folks. It's said you have a special dislike for aging Indians."

For some reason, the captain was stopped in his tracks by what Rusty said. He looked around him like for the first time and noticed all the Indians staring at him with tombstones in their eyes. He saw the privates were just as scared of him as they were the Indians—maybe more. They were both shivering from the nearing chilly evening and the fear they felt to the core of their very being.

Captain Holmes looked across the faces as he blinked his eyes like he was trying to remove the cobwebs. He was so furious and so close to capturing the deserters, he was in a world of his own. It was something that happened to him more and more often in moments of pressure or danger. It was one reason he was so effective. It made him ruthless in times when such actions were needed.

Or at least those were the orders he received, and he willingly, even happily, carried them out to the letter, killing every heathen regardless of age or sex. They were all to be eliminated—especially women and young boys. The women would have more offspring, increasing the size of the tribe, and the boys would soon grow into men and more warriors. It was simple, really. The captain believed if you wanted to eliminate a race of people, the only way to do it was to be as thorough as possible. He felt his plan was the only thing that would work.

As far as the two deserters, it was true: they killed their lieutenant and ran from the Army. Both offenses required either the noose or a firing squad as far as Army law dictated. The situation escalated when the captain reported the killing to the local mayor. How could they allow two lowly soldiers to kill an officer and get away with it, not to mention the desertion?

After some convincing, Captain Holmes talked the mayor into putting up a thousand dollars each as a reward. The dead lieutenant came from the same town, and he convinced him it would be a blemish on the city's record if they were allowed to vanish without paying for their wicked deeds.

Everything before he got there nearly fell into place on its own. When the opportunity arose, Holmes stood up and was willing and ready. His commander blessed him to chase after the deserters, the marshal was made an offer he couldn't refuse, and along he came too. The major admonished him for going with so few men, so Holmes requested a leave of duty so he could pursue the bounties. He did so with his commanding officer's unofficial blessing. They both knew what he planned, and the major approved.

The four men were dragged into the large lodge. The only light came from the open door and a fire at either end as the men filed in; the sun began to drop off the edge of the world where a battle ensued, staining the sky with a multitude of colors. The dark of night came suddenly with the chatter of crickets. The air smelled of wood fires and tobacco.

Rusty, Levi, and Will ducked their heads to enter the lodge—Johnson was so wide he entered sideways. They had to let their eyes adjust to the dimness. The four prisoners were at one end of the lodge, and the elders and chiefs at the other. The few allowed to observe sat in the middle with Rusty and his friends. Some sat on the other side of the fire as the flames' shadows danced on the teepee walls.

The room was just as serious as any hearing they had ever seen—maybe even more so. The elders would be the jury, and the war chief the prosecutor. The trespassers would represent themselves. It was they who trespassed, so they would be allowed to plead for their lives. They had them lined up, with Todd Zillow and Jimmy Jones first, then the marshal, and last came Captain Holmes. He wore a scowl of disrespect on his face.

No matter how much danger he was in, he still acted belligerently. He must have thought he was indestructible or unkillable. It was apparent he still didn't believe he would die at the hands of the hostiles. It was like he still couldn't figure out why they didn't fear him like everybody else he had met in the past. Then again, he had never been in an Indian camp when he wasn't slaughtering the tribe. Then it was full of screams, and the acrid smell of blood seemed dense in the air. Now, the only screams were in the privates' minds.

Rusty Steel spoke Crow as well as Hachta spoke English. They decided they would both be translators, so there was a White man and an Indian repeating the words in a different language. This would ensure they both translated the same thing. Chato motioned for the first White man to be brought before the elders. Hachta stood, stared at the young soldier, and smiled to help him relax. Both privates were nearly incoherent from fear. The smile reached the war chief's eyes, and Todd Zillow calmed enough to breathe deeply and maybe try to answer some questions.

"Did you have permission from a Crow chief to come to our land?" Hachta translated from the first elder.

"No, sir," Todd said. "I'm not allowed to decide where I wanna go. I'm given orders and do what I'm told —at least every time but that last one. Jimmy and I didn't want to obey the captain's last orders. That was just before we run off."

"Did you kill your officer as accused?" Hachta asked.

"Yes, sir, we did," Todd replied. "But only after they pointed a gun at us, intending to shoot. We were only defending ourselves. I knew just the same the Army ain't gonna want to know about anything but the lieutenant and us denying to follow orders."

"There is one more question the chief wants to ask you, Todd Zillow," Hachta said, speaking slowly, so he was understood.

"Have you ever killed Crow Indians?" Hachta asked. His eyes narrowed, and his brow furrowed as he waited for the answer.

"Yes, sir, I've kilt seven in the year I've been attached to the Indian wars."

A murmur ripped through those present when he translated the last question. Their eyes shot daggers at the White man.

"You call this the Indian wars?" Hachta asked. "Is that the official name in Washington?"

"Yes, sir, it's as official as anything that comes directly from Congress."

"And these Indians you killed," Hachta asked, "were they old people and women?"

"No, sir, they weren't," Todd replied. "Jimmy and I don't kill no women or children. That was the order we nearly got shot for disobeying. We were ordered to kill everybody we found in the village. When we asked the lieutenant about the old folks and wives, he said everybody was to be shot, or stabbed when possible, to save gunpowder. There must have been maybe fifty people in all. Of that, there were some seventeen or eighteen warriors. We went through the braves like butter but refused to kill their wives, mothers, daughters, sons, and parents. A man has to draw a line someplace, even if it puts his life in peril. I reckon we're a perfect example of that."

The elders murmured among themselves, and the chief even put his two cents in. Hachta patiently waited; he had no more questions for Todd Zillow. He was ready for the next prisoner.

"We're done with him," Chief Chato said. "Bring the second man to be questioned."

Jimmy Wilson wasn't as brave as Todd. He couldn't get his chin to stop quivering the whole time he stood before the heads of the tribe. He had always heard of the terrible things the Indians did to White people. He had always been told to shoot himself before allowing his capture. He stood before the tribe's leaders, shaking like a leaf. Hachta smiled, but his face twisted up and made him look gruesome, so Jimmy became more frightened. He could hardly get a word to come out at first. He opened and closed his mouth like a beached bass gulping for air.

"What is your name, bluecoat?" Hachta asked.

"James Butler Wilson, but everybody calls me Jimmy."

"Are you an Army chief?" Hachta asked.

"An Army chief?" James replied. "As far as I know, we don't have no chiefs."

"He means officers," Rusty Steel intervened.

If looks could kill, Captain Holmes would have had

Mr. Steel dead in his sights, but Rusty ignored him. He had seen men like Holmes in the past. They only thought about themselves and were always at odds with everybody.

"Me—an officer?" Jimmy asked, surprised. "I reckon not, sir. I ain't been in the Army a year yet, sir."

"So, you were not the man who gave Private Zillow the order to kill everyone in the village?" Hachta asked. "Women and children included?"

"Why, I wouldn't know how to officer a bunch of men on patrol. I wouldn't even know where to start, and I'm danged sure I ain't ever given any orders to anybody. Todd and me are the bottom men on the totem pole, so we only get orders and don't give 'em."

"Is it true you and your friend refused to act on these orders?" Hachta asked, carefully selecting his words. The eyes of the elders fell on Jimmy, making him nervous all over again.

"Are ya gonna kill us?" Jimmy asked. A single tear ran down his cheek.

"Just answer the question truthfully, and we will see," Hachta replied.

"Yes, sir," Jimmy said. "We refused to act on the lieutenant's orders to kill everybody in the village, just like Todd said. We're soldiers and kill folks in the war like everybody does, but we ain't murderers. At least we weren't until Todd shot the lieutenant. I ain't pushing the blame on him because I had my gun out, and I fired too. He just beat me to it. He was gonna kill us without a court-martial or anything. He said we were disobeying orders in times of war."

"And these orders were to kill women, children, and our elders, is that correct, Private?" Hachta asked.

Jimmy looked down at the ground, made a hole in the dirt with his shoe, and his shoulders slumped. He couldn't meet Hachta's eyes when he replied, "Yes, sir, they were. When I thought about it, all I could see was my ma, sisters, and grandpa. I just didn't have it in me. I reckon I wasn't cut out to be a soldier at the end, now was I?"

Hachta translated, and even though Rusty and he had been friends for years and he had lived in a Crow camp, he made sure every word was what the private said and nothing more or less. Talking about something in Crow was complicated. The wrong word could make everything mean something different.

The elders nodded, and Chief Chato waved his hand to take the second prisoner away. He dragged his feet with every step, like his boots weighed fifty pounds.

"Before we continue, the elders want us to have a word alone," Hachta said. "Please wait outside, Rusty. My braves will take the prisoners out." He turned his eyes on the captain and the marshal. "If I were you two, I would behave myself, because my warriors have already heard enough to take at least the captain's scalp, and I can't guarantee they won't get carried away."

The blood drained from Marshal Jack Wilson's face. He knew he was next and would rather get it out of the way than prolong it with nonsense. The Indian ways were unacceptable. Who ever heard of them putting White men on trial? They just didn't understand they were an inferior race. The confidence he'd had up till now seemed to falter. He had been sure they wouldn't mess with a US Marshal. But if the fact be known, he, too, was a murderer. Right now, he'd just as soon shoot both chiefs and be done with it, but they had taken away their guns.

That security he felt that they wouldn't kill a marshal began to evaporate. Now, he realized that just being with Captain Holmes was enough to have him executed. He was guilty of killing women and children. Wilson wondered: if he had to, could he kill a woman? Even Marshal Jack Wilson had his boundaries, which the captain obviously didn't.

THE SOLDIERS

"WHATCHA THINK THEY'RE GONNA DO, RUSTY?" LEVI asked as soon as they walked out into the night. "It was mighty tense in there."

Lightning bugs flashed in the dark, then disappeared, only to light up somewhere else. A dozen fires crackled within hearing distance, and the smell of grilled meat floated on puffs of air. The tribe appeared to have returned to everyday life, but the White men could see them sneak looks at the prisoners. Their eyes shot daggers at the soldiers, although they seemed somewhat indifferent to the marshal.

They hadn't heard of marshals killing Indians other than in town hangings. Hachta believed those Indians deserved it for abandoning their tribe. They didn't seem to notice the mountain men. This was something that aggravated Captain Holmes to no end. He knew they were Indian lovers. It was obvious.

"You're in cahoots with these stinking Injuns, aren't you, old fool?" Captain Holmes spat. "If I had you down from this mountain, I'd have you given a hundred lashes."

"Have you been ordering that invisible army of yours around again, Captain?" Rusty asked and laughed. "I'm afraid that the only one that seems to see it is you. Now that makes you the old fool, don't it? You're the one all tied up and on trial for killing Indians."

"There's no law against killing Indians," Holmes spat. "Especially for an officer and a gentleman."

"You may be an officer, which makes me fear our country is doomed if they have men like you runnin' our army," Rusty said. "But you sure as hell ain't a gentleman, pardon my French. Now ya see how you affect good people like me. I'm not a man to swear. You bring the bad out in everybody you meet, Captain." His eyes shifted accusingly at the marshal, who couldn't hold eye contact with Rusty Steel.

"Whatcha think is gonna happen?" Levi whispered as they separated themselves from the prisoners and the tribespeople. "I don't see any way this will come out without bloodshed."

"So, now that the Indians are shedding the blood, it's somehow different?" Rusty asked. "What do you think that officer was gonna do to the privates and every Indian he ran into on the way? That's his job, Levi. He signed on and got a salary for killing people with red skin, no matter how old they are or whether they are men or women."

"They'd shoot them as soon as they arrived at the fort in Leavenworth, Kansas," Will Forrester said. "The court-martial would be rudimentary and just going through the steps for the show and politics. As far as the

Army is concerned, they have already been declared guilty of disobeying an order and killing their commanding officer. Maybe in a civil court of law, they wouldn't be hanged. It would depend on the jury. Civilians don't like murdering women and children, no matter whether they are Black, White, or Red. But there's only one outcome for such acts of disobedience in a military court: a firing squad."

"I know it sounds bad, but did you hear what their orders were?" Levi huffed. "We can't allow people to go around killing women and children, no matter what color they be."

"I have to stand by Levi on this one," Rusty said. "I think what's wrong is you've still got too much military runnin' through your veins for your own good."

"I've felt that myself lately," Will admitted. He felt so relaxed with his friends that he opened up, which was unusual for the ex-Army captain. "To be honest, I feel intimidated by the captain. We're even the same rank, and still, I feel he'll start bullying me at any moment. I don't even like being around him, but at the same time, I can understand where he is coming from. He has been trained to fight Indians for so many years I'm sure he's lost account. It's the longest-lasting war in American history and has no signs of ending anytime soon."

"That's why they're going for the women and children," Forrester said. "The women won't have babies, and their children won't grow up to fight White men. They look at the big picture when the Indians no longer roam free. I believe it's inevitable, no matter how terrible it sounds. People are coming west by the hoards from all over America and Europe. The East Coast is already densely populated. I studied back East at West

Point. You have to go to St. Louis to find the beginning of the wilderness."

"We all know how dangerous Kansas is," Rusty harrumphed. "Those same evil people will come farther west to run from the law as civilization nears the Indians' homes and the plains with the buffalo. I've heard the plans from the top in Washington. The first step is to wipe out the buffalo. Then the Indians will have no food or hides to make their homes. This will change their lives forever."

"You sure do paint a dark future," Levi huffed. "I hope it don't happen in our lifetimes. I'm just beginning to learn to live up here, and I love it. We can always go out and explore. You could even map the Rocky Mountains. Just because you're not Army anymore don't mean you can't complete your dream. You studied geography to discover trails and forge through the wilderness, didn't cha? Now you have the opportunity. Forget the Army. Like I said back at the cabin, maybe we should stop sticking our noses in other peoples' business. Especially in such a delicate situation."

Just being near an Army officer affected Will Forrester. Holmes had even recognized his picture from the big to-do they made on their departure. Unfortunately for Will, it had made the first page. At one time, he would have been prouder of that than anything in the world. He wondered what was really printed in the newspapers in the end. After they found out what happened, maybe it would be better if he didn't know.

"Whatcha think they're gonna do with us, Mister Steel?" Todd Zillow asked. "Are they gonna do the things I read in the newspapers? You know, torture? I ain't all that afraid of dying. Being in the Army and all, you get used to death. But you expect it to be a bullet or arrow to the heart or the head. I never thought I would end up over a fire or whatever they plan to do to us. The sad thing is, I reckon they got every right to do it too. We should have never tried to hide in the Rocky Mountains. We thought the threat of Indians would scare the Army off."

"From what I've seen, they ain't much scared of nothin', let alone us," Jimmy Jones said. "They sure as the dickens ain't scared of the captain, and everybody is afraid of Captain Holmes."

"You just think everybody's afraid of Captain Holmes," Levi said. "I think he's the one that's afraid, and he tries to hide it by bullying people. But us mountain men don't bully."

Jimmy looked from Levi to Rusty and said, "You didn't answer my question. You know—what's the Crow Indians gonna do to us after the trial?"

Rusty looked at him surprised and replied, "Why, I have no idea. I'm as excited as you to hear the verdict, but we've got to get through the second half of the trial first."

"You've gotta tell me," Jimmy insisted. He looked like his nerves were shattered. His eyes were bouncing around like Mexican jumping beans.

"The only one I'm pretty sure about is the captain," Rusty said. "He ain't got a shot in the dark to make it out of the stronghold alive. I don't like it any more than you do, but we ain't the law up here. The Crow, Blackfeet, Sioux, and Ute are. We're just guests here, and you best feel lucky to be here. Now you can see what they do to most White folks that mosey over this way if they don't kill 'em straight off. The Crow didn't even have to hunt your bunch. Y'all fell right into their arms."

"We didn't fall into anybody's arms," Captain Holmes growled. "We fell into a cleverly planned trap."

"So, you've already rationalized all the sliding and tumbling down the cliff right into the arms of the waiting Crow?" Rusty asked. "They knew you were comin' an hour before you got here."

"How would you know what the Indians were doing?" Holmes asked as he eyed Rusty Steel suspiciously. "You arrived right after we did, but not before."

"You were bein' watched a long time before you rolled into the camp." Rusty laughed. "We were waitin' and watching you four. I thank ya kindly for providin' us a good spell of entertainment. I like to get as much as I can. The Crow was probably following y'all since you started up the hill. You can't fart up here without a Crow Indian getting wind of it." He laughed until he got a stitch.

"If I get out of this, I'm going to see you hang," Captain Holmes growled.

"And how is that gonna work out, mister know-it-all?" Rusty asked. His face was red from laughing.

The captain's eyes drilled holes into Rusty, but he completely ignored the captain. This just made the officer angrier. He had never been spoken to in such a way; indeed, he'd never been tied up. The Crow tied only the thumbs together. This ensured their digits fell asleep and began to throb and ache. It was much less comfortable than tying a man's wrists.

"I don't know how I'm going to do it, but I promise you, you'll die before I do," Captain Holmes said.

Everybody looked at the lodge door when Hachta

walked out. His face was a mask of neutrality. There wasn't a hint of how he felt one way or another. He didn't even appear angry in the face of Captain Holmes.

The same elders were present, but two medicine men were there this time too. There were dozens of braids in their hair. They wore wolf and coyote head-dresses, necklaces from bear claws, and feathers hanging from their earlobes.

"Marshal Jack Wilson," Hachta said slowly, so he was clear and concise.

He was a methodical man who missed little. He wasn't the chief, much to his displeasure, but he still held great power in the tribe as the head war chief. He was always in control and never faltered. He was the camp's most reliable man, including the new chief, and Chato knew it. He even resented it a little. Hachta would always have to walk lightly and beware of traps.

He was lucky the tribe loved him, so it would be dangerous for the big chief to kill or banish him from the tribe. Still, Hachta remained a constant threat to the actual chief. Sure, he was the old chief's son-in-law, but his wife's father suddenly got sick and died in only three days.

He had felt the tension with the elders when they were alone in the lodge. It was as if Chato was disputing everything he said. Finally, Hachta had stopped talking to keep the peace. He was brave enough to accept the situation and move on.

"What do you think the Crow Indians are gonna do to me?" Marshal Wilson asked. "If the truth be known, I'm no more than an observer. I came along to officially arrest the prisoners."

"And why couldn't the captain take 'em back?" Rusty

asked. "Two privates shouldn't propose much of a challenge to a captain so well known for killin' folks."

"Oh, he was gonna keep 'em in the end," Marshal Wilson said. "I had to arrest 'im first to get the bounty money."

"Something don't add up here," Levi said. "Is that how the Army works, Will?"

"How much bounty money were you going to get?" Forrester asked.

"Five hundred dollars," the marshal blurted.

"Shut your mouth, fool," Captain Holms spat. "The marshal is just as implicated as I am in the bounty money. It might be a stretch, but it ain't illegal. I'm on unpaid leave. It's like I wasn't even in the Army. I'm just as innocent as Marshal Wilson."

"Oh, I doubt the marshal is innocent at all," Levi said. "I passed through Kansas on my way here and saw little resembling law and order. I heard most lawmen this far west were outlaws before that. That's what brings so many vermin west."

"Everybody back inside," Hachta ordered.

A half dozen warriors made sure the reluctant and belligerent Holmes cooperated. Still, the fury inside the Army captain boiled. He seemed to get angrier and angrier with every confrontation and every time he spoke.

Rusty spread a grin across his cheeks, nearly touching his eyes as they twinkled with mischief. He was having a grand time observing the follies of humankind at its dumbest. He was amazed this captain survived this long. His ideas were appalling to all three mountain men. There was no need to fight with the Indians. The eight men living in the compound had proved that White men and the Crow could live together in harmony. He felt part Crow himself from the years he had lived with a tribe of the Crow Nation along with Flathead Indians.

They filed into the room. The smoke was dense, and their eyes stung until they became accustomed. Embers glowed orange on the Indians' faces, making them appear more ancient than they were. Deep shadows pronounced their wrinkles, which were like roadmaps of a town.

The four prisoners were seated as before, and they stared straight ahead. Hachta walked to the marshal and grabbed his arm to lift him. He walked into the lodge with the elders, and they began with the questions. But even though Wilson tried to convince them he wasn't a bounty hunter, they decided he made his living trading flesh for cash—one of the lowest forms of life in the mountains and the plains.

"You can sit down, Marshal Wilson," Hachta said. "We already know who you are."

MARSHAL WILSON

"So, THIS IS THE FAMOUS CAVALRYMAN, CAPTAIN Holmes," Hachta said. "I have heard about you in the Indian gossip. Where are the children's and women's scalps? Or is that something that the heathens do but not you, the murder of our mothers and babies?"

"You've already made up your mind about what you're going to do," Holmes growled. "Why the three-ring circus? I ain't afraid of you redskins." He turned to Hachta and said, "Maybe I'll take you out before you get me. If I die, you die too."

"You're right, we have decided what to do to you—ultimately," Hachta said. "What we are deciding now is the how and the duration. If you keep flapping your mouth, we may decide sooner. I am not afraid of death either, but I don't taunt it like you, Captain Holmes. You are the fool here for not seeing your actual situation. Only an ignoramus taunts death. Look at Marshal Wilson there. He isn't fooling himself. He has accepted whatever is to come."

"Don't you believe for a minute he isn't as guilty as

me," Holmes said. "If I am guilty, as you say, he must be too. Yet you treat him with more respect and taunt me to anger with your mind games. I challenge you to a duel."

Hachta looked at Rusty, puzzled, and raised an eyebrow. "What does this word duel mean?"

"That's a fancy way to say he wants to fight ya," Levi said. "I reckon it means to the death too. Most duels I've heard of are with pistols. If I'm not mistaken, the one challenged is the one who picks the weapons."

"You aren't thinking of fighting this fool, are you?" Rusty said. "He doesn't deserve the honor of fighting you."

Everybody looked at the White men and then back at Hachta. Chato was talking and wanted to discuss the torture, but the Army captain and his war chief had stolen his thunder. Now everybody was looking at them and not at him. Everybody in the camp knew both men and was aware of their rivalry.

With Chato, even his name was against him and had always made life difficult. It meant short. To add insult to injury, he was five-four. That didn't mean he wasn't a fighter, because he had been a warrior like Hachta before his father-in-law died.

Chato pushed Hachta aside and said, "I will fight the White man. I will show you who the champion of the tribe is. After today, it will be clear I deserve the position of chief, if anyone had any doubts. This wasn't given to me because I was the chief's son-in-law but because I deserved it. I am entitled to be chief and will prove it to all our Crow people." His stare bore holes into Hachta, but he was too shocked to take offense.

"Chief Chato," Hachta said, horrified. "We can't risk the life of our chief. I will fight the captain. You can kill him quickly if he wins, so he doesn't suffer. If he loses, he will die for five days—he will lose one limb every day, and on the fifth day, he will lose his head. That is, if we can keep him alive after the fight. It's best to start with the legs while the body is still strong. Then, hopefully, he will survive."

"I don't like you putting words in my mouth," Chato spat. "I'll fight the captain and decide what happens to him too. You can make a judgment on the two lowly soldiers. They are not famous and are of no importance to me. Do you really think a White soldier can beat me? Don't you remember who I am? I was always right behind you at archery, tomahawks, knives, and mortal combat. Then I passed your skills, and now I am chief, and you aren't. You better keep this clear in your mind and don't forget. One day I might not be so forgiving."

Hachta's eyes blazed red as his blood boiled. He held his tongue—his mouth was a brutal, angry gash. He wanted to strangle Chato with his bare hands, but he was a warrior and a war chief, so he had to continue with the proper protocol—the way honorable men deal with situations. He broke off his fiery gaze and averted his eyes passively.

He didn't want to kill Chato. They had been friends until they began to compete as warriors. He was a great warrior but too egotistical to rule their people. He also was under the impression that he was much better than he was—something that was not lost on Hachta. A leader must be fierce and humble, depending on what the situation called for. Now he humbled himself before his chief and the tribe.

"Let the games begin," Chief Chato cried out to the cheers of the tribe. "The first two White men who survive may be given a chance to flee. That will be the privates. The winner wins the right to attempt to escape my warriors—the losers will die at the tribe's hands. They will be given a half day lead. Then we will go after them, but first, you must defeat my braves, man-to-man. The first two will fight weaponless. This is not about death but about honor and bravery. Then my war chief, Hachta, will fight the marshal." He looked at Hachta, and a slight grin of pleasure crossed his lips before the chief had time to hide it. He was risking his life for his pride when he should have been thinking about the tribe rather than himself.

"Finally, it will be the cruel captain's turn, this man they call *Captain Holmes the Butcher* among the Indian tribes. Then he and I will fight with knives. First, the privates will fight the warriors Hachta matches up. Then the war chief will fight the marshal, and finally, I will fight and defeat the Army captain who likes to kill women, children, and grandparents. It will be my pleasure to end his life. The elders have decided this, so this is how it will be."

"Forgive me, Chief, but you shouldn't take such risks," Hachta said humbly. "Fighting White soldiers man-to-man is not work for a chief. It is the job of the war chief."

"I know you wanted to be chief," Chato whispered. "My wife's father made me chief. This is final, and still, you plot to go against me. I will not let you be our people's champion again and steal my thunder. Stand aside and do as you're told."

"I'll do no such thing," Hachta said. "I am here to comply with your wishes and keep you safe. You know I wanted to be chief, and I knew you wanted the same thing. It is normal that one of us loses. I am disappointed that I was not chosen, but I am a warrior and accept defeat just like I rejoice in victory. Let me fight the marshal and the captain too. This way, you will see I am faithful to my tribe and its leader regardless of who is selected. For me, it was not meant to be."

Chato looked at his war chief, and he still felt threatened. He believed Hachta's desire to lead the tribe was above all things, like it was for him. He'd never realized that Hachta believed only honor and loyalty were more important than being chief. Without either, you would ultimately fail as a leader. With the hordes of White people at their doors and more coming all the time, the tribe needed a solid chief in whom they could have confidence.

But Chato felt that if he allowed Hachta to fight and beat the marshal and the captain, he would lose face in front of the warriors and his people. He must conquer the captain alone to show he was a strong chief and leader. Time would tell how his war chief fared against the marshal.

He had heard the stories about the violence the captain had wreaked on unsuspecting tribes, but he wondered how he fought when it was a Crow warrior, and chief no less, and hand-to-hand. He wouldn't be fighting the elders, women, and children this time. Now, he would be fighting an actual Crow warrior. Nor would he have twenty men to back him up. He would be fighting all alone. Still, the arrogance of the man angered the Crow chief. Only one warrior sort of understood him.

Hachta knew this was about honor and his word more than his life because he was clearly willing to forfeit them were it for the better of the tribe and their honor. If he died today, he might become a martyr. Then he would have the respect of many men there in the mountains. That was why he was willing to die fighting. He knew one day, these wars would be lost to the White man, and he dreaded the day. The same could be said for the war chief.

Hachta selected two of his youngest warriors to fight with the two lowly soldiers. He wanted to pick men who were equals or even inferior. It would be a good lesson for his braves, and it might save the lives of the privates. They'd never harmed any innocent Crow Indians, but they would have to flee far away and never come back here again nor speak of the place. Of course, they would remain wanted, so their only escape was to leave the country. Hachta even hoped that Zillow and Wilson would win so they would have a chance to survive and live—as long as they never returned to these mountains. There would be conditions.

Todd and Jimmy were as nervous as a cat in a room full of rocking chairs. They were faced off with two Indian boys that seemed a few years younger than them, and they weren't old by any stretch of the imagination. Now, these new warriors would know what a battle was with experienced soldiers or warriors. Both would be suitable lessons. It was not the same as fighting a Blackfoot Indian.

Happy and Gray Fox stood expressionless as they faced the two young soldiers. None of them had weapons and were to fight until two men gave up. Which two would it be? Would the Army soldiers easily defeat the young sixteen-year-old warriors, or would the young, healthy specimens tear them to pieces? All eyes turned toward Chief Chato for the signal to begin.

Todd and Jimmy were pushed inside the ring made for the games. Sixty warrior braves circled the men, so there was no escape. Their Indian opponents dropped low and circled the puzzled privates. They knew they had to win, but what would they get in return? A prolonged death? Still, they would fight as long as they could. While they had the strength to fight, there was still hope, even though the only light they saw at the end of the tunnel was from a big, black Baldwin locomotive.

Todd and Jimmy had fought against Indians many times before. They hadn't been in the Army all that long, but they were sent straight to the frontier, where the Indian wars were. So, they weren't foreign to action but were confused by the need. They supposed they were making a mockery of them by pairing them with opponents that would beat them soundly.

But when the fight started, they could tell it was mismatched. The soldiers were young, but still, they were twice the size of the youthful warriors and had plenty of experience. As soon as the Indians got near the soldiers, they threw dirt in their faces and kicked them so hard between the legs their eyes nearly popped out. The roaring crowd went silent. None of them expected it to be so short.

Two young braves rolled in the dirt, their hands between their legs moaning. The hard Army boot toes put them down, and they weren't getting back up anytime soon. Hachta stifled a chuckle—he didn't want his students to think it was funny. Now, they would realize just how much they needed to learn before facing Army soldiers and surviving. It was wise of Hachta to teach all the young warriors a lesson. It is essential to know your enemy. That was why he learned English.

"Did we already win?" Jimmy asked, confused. He wasn't sure what the rules were or what they were to do, but the young Indians were done for the day. They couldn't believe how easily the soldiers defeated the braves.

Rusty shot a knowing look at his friend Hachta. He had taken a bad situation and turned it into a lesson for his men. Most chiefs would only see the opportunity for vengeance. The Crow war chief saw the big picture.

"They cheated us," Gray Fox groaned as he wiggled on the ground like a worm.

"I give up," Happy said as he rocked back and forth from the pain.

"They didn't cheat you," Hachta said. "They beat you fair and square. Nobody said anything about rules. The only rule was guns or knives were not allowed so that you would be equally matched. I only said to win—I didn't say how, and you failed miserably. Throwing dirt in your eyes was the oldest trick I know. You both should have been ready. Now you know that when you stalk White trespassers in the wilderness, they may be as dangerous as you—maybe more. Don't think you can beat a man until you have done so."

When the privates returned and took a seat near Rusty, Todd looked at him and asked, "What just happened?"

"That's a fool question." Rusty laughed. "Ain't that apparent? You and your buddy Jimmy won the fight, although that don't mean you've won the war."

"The war?" Todd asked, more perplexed than before. "I don't know why they don't get on with it and kill us."

"Never give up, pard," Rusty whispered. "Maybe you'll get a chance to run off. If I was you, I'd pick Canada. There ain't no US lawmen can go there and bring ya back. Change your names and run north while ya got a chance. That's what I'd do."

"What's he talkin' about?" Jimmy asked his friend. "Our gooses are already cooked, and he's talking about settling in another country. I don't see how we're gonna get out of the spot we're in."

"I think everybody up here is plumb crazy if you ask me," Todd huffed. "Now we have to wait to see what else they've got in store for us before they kill us. I've always heard it takes days to torture a man to death."

"Hush up, you pups," Marshal Wilson spat. He was fed up and ready for a fight. "Spit in their eye and take it like a grown-up. We're dead already anyway."

Jack had been tied up, poked with a stick, spat on, and an Indian had even urinated on his boots. He was tired, sore, and at the end of his rope. He was ready for a good scrap, and the Indian making all the noise was standing there, chuckling.

"I'm gonna wipe that smile right off your face, fool," Marshal Wilson spat. "I ain't no Indian fighter, but I've killed a man or two, and now I'm gonna kill you."

The marshal moved around the ring of humanity and twirled his fists like a prizefighter. Hachta just stood there with a mask for a face. He made no move to defend himself. Jack steeled his resolve and made a pass at the large Indian. He swung for his jaw with a big haymaker. If it found its mark, it would knock a man's head off.

He swung, but the War Chief Hachta wasn't there anymore. Now he was standing three feet away. Jack hadn't even seen him move. He must have slipped out of the way when Jack pulled back to send him to the moon. He knew if he made contact, it would be all she wrote.

He's a sneaky one, but he's runnin' scared, Marshal Wilson thought. *He don't even know how to fight like a man.*

The marshal circled the war chief, and all Hachta did was gracefully spin on his heel as he kept his eyes focused on his opponent. He would bide his time until the right moment arose.

Two jabs and an uppercut whooshed through the air, but all three swings missed their mark. Hachta hadn't seemed even to have moved—he was still in the same place. His eyes were hooded, and his face had changed to a mask of danger. It was as though another person was emerging. This was not the same man who started the fight. This one was the essence of a warrior. His focus took in everything around him—all sights, sounds, and even the pressure of the air. He was detached from the fight but used his mind to create the illusion that he was in one place when he was already moving to another. It was a movement so quick Marshal Wilson couldn't see it.

The confidence drained from Jack's face like blood. He suddenly realized his mistake. He thought this was just another one of the Indians they found on the trail. Now, he realized he was very wrong. There was something special about this warrior. The marshal knew he was up against a much more challenging man than he expected. Now, he had to pull out all the stops and play dirty. He was looking for any opportunity.

He tried the same trick as the privates, but before he could throw the dirt in Hachta's face, he had already covered his eyes. No matter what he did, he seemed just as calm as when he walked into the ring of warriors. Jack was huffing and puffing, out of breath, and the war chief breathed like he was asleep—long, deep, calm breaths. The marshal's face glistened with sweat, and his shirt stuck to his back. Hachta was as cool as a winter's spring.

Jack Wilson's eyes flashed everywhere, expecting something to come at him from some unexpected direction. His confidence faded like a wilted flower. Even his courage and brash, foolish behavior faltered and stalled. He knew now that if he didn't reach way down inside, pull out his last bit of grit, and face this terrifying man, he wouldn't make it. He didn't even get excited enough to sweat.

Marshal Jack Wilson reassessed the situation. He used his peripheral vision as he looked for something to grab. There had to be something there to give him an advantage. The crowd of Crow Indians roared behind him. It was almost as frightening as the war chief before him. He suddenly felt claustrophobic as the crowd pressed in. Everywhere he looked, he saw eyes boring into his. He was getting lightheaded and knew he had to find something to fight with. He suddenly remembered his belt. The buckle held a small knife when pulled out. It wasn't much, but it might turn the tide if he could get close.

He hadn't considered what the tribe would do to

him if he did kill their war chief. This was supposed to be a fight for honor, and the first two contestants weren't killed, so maybe there was no reason to believe anyone would die here. But the marshal's survival instincts kicked in, and they believed all people thought like him.

All men were wicked and would commit murder if it was dangled before their faces long enough. Jack Wilson hadn't hesitated when it came time to kill a man. He wasn't proud of it, but it didn't bother him either. It was just another page in the book of his life. There were several killings in the end—before and after he had a badge to make it legal.

Jack crouched as he slipped his belt from his pants. In one smooth motion, he used it like a whip. This time Hachta wasn't fast enough, and a welt and cut sprouted instantly on his cheek. The Indian touched his face and the blood, then tasted it—he smiled. It was like he said maybe there was more to the White marshal than he thought.

When he exposed the knife, sunrays flashed off the blade. Hachta frowned, and a murmur rumbled through the crowd of warriors. But Chief Chato didn't mention the infraction of the rules of the game. The marshal had just made this a real fight.

When the White man circled, Hachta planted his pivot foot firmly and moved with him. He slowly moved around the fighting circle; each man was looking for that opportunity. Jack's eyes were the color of blood, and white foam showed at the edges of his mouth. Hachta could tell by his body language when he would strike next. He knew he would make two or three strikes with the knife when he charged and they got close.

Hachta had to keep sharp to avoid the knife. He

knew his opponent was already a dead man walking for breaking the rules. If only he had played fairly, maybe all he would have gotten was a sound beating. Now, he had made it personal when it was only supposed to be a game. Now, it was for keeps. Even if he managed to kill Hachta, his warriors would tear him to pieces for breaking the rules.

"This was supposed to have been a game," Hachta whispered to his opponent. "Now that you've made it personal, make sure you don't hold back. I plan to give you no chances, Marshal."

Across the camp, smoke squirreled into the sky, but still the women and children hid from the Army captain. The only sound was the camp dogs, who were barking fiercely. They were tied to a post at the back of the camp. They howled and yapped. They knew something was wrong.

Jack flicked his belt and got out of the way just in time, but it was a trick. When Hachta dodged the belt, he didn't see the knife as a clean slice appeared in his shirt, soaked with blood. Hachta ignored his injury. Whether it be minor or severe, he couldn't stop to check now. A man with a knife was trying to kill him.

The marshal seemed to have the upper hand. Of course, he wasn't playing by the rules, but he figured he was a dead man anyway, so he would go out fighting. Maybe by some stroke of luck, he might be able to kill the war chief. That would be a spit in their eyes, even though he knew what would follow. He growled and moved in for the kill.

Two flicks of the leather belt with a thin tip cracked Hachta's face making two deep cuts. Blood flowed freely down his cheeks to drip off his chin. Drops turned into rivulets of claret. Marshal Jack Wilson knew it was time. It was now or never. He went in for the kill. This time Hachta didn't even move. Everything slowed down like it did in times of violence. The blade was headed for just under his ribcage. The Indian could see the movements as he played them out in his mind. He waited as the blade raced for his body.

The knuckle punch to the marshal's neck sucked all his wind. Hachta heard his windpipe break. It sounded like breaking dry branches. Now, he lay on the ground, unable to breathe. He made big gasps for air, but little oxygen got through. The Crow war chief didn't even look at Wilson. He turned and took his place beside the chief.

"The White marshal lacked respect for our tribe by using the knife and injuring Hachta!" Chato yelled. "The marshal understood it was against the rules. No one was to die yet." The chief spat in the dirt and said, "Kill him at once!"

The marshal still struggled desperately to breathe, so he didn't hear what the chief said. In a second, he was so full of holes from lances he looked like a human pincushion. When the warriors backed away to create a human circle again, two Indians had the marshal by the feet as they dragged the lifeless body out of the ring.

"This man died for nothing," Hachta called out. "He broke the rules of the games. This was not about death until the marshal made it personal. Now, he dies for breaking his word, trespassing on our land, and selling flesh for money."

He looked across the crowd at his young and old warriors, hoping they were taught some lesson in the marshal's actions. Now they had to deal with the captain, who would be a real Indian fighter. Hachta didn't believe he should speak out more about Chato fighting the captain. If he said something now, he might dishonor him before the tribe. Hachta knew he had to bite his tongue and refrain from further discussion. Obviously, the chief felt threatened by his war chief. He saw it in his face and heard it in his voice. He averted his eyes to the ground and fell silent.

CHIEF CHATO

AFTER THE MARSHAL'S BODY WAS DRAGGED AWAY, IT vanished behind the crowd. You could see a slight sign of relief from the two privates. They had dodged yet another bullet and were still alive with one enemy less. Now came the captain, though. Of course, they came from the same outpost, so they knew of his reputation. He hated Indians with such a passion that he went over and beyond the call of duty to try to eliminate the race single-handedly. Both privates knew the Indians had heard some of the stories, but if they knew had known what the privates knew, they would have slit his throat then and there.

He had lined tribes up, telling them they were taking them to a better place to live where they wouldn't want for food or a home. They walked along a trail submissively, allowing the Army to lead them to a reservation. They had so little food they thought perhaps they would eat better with the rich White people who had everything. When they arrived at the place where the valley ended in a cliff, straight down three hundred feet, Captain Holmes had the bugler sound out the orders, and twenty soldiers attacked the defenseless Indians with rifles and pistols. When they ran out of bullets, they used their bayonets on the muskets to finish them off. The ones that didn't die at the top were dead by the time they hit bottom.

They pushed them off the cliff to the bottom of a ravine. Their bodies were hidden in the brush. Todd and Jimmy remembered their shock when the captain had ordered these Indians killed. There wasn't a single man the age of a warrior. The captain did it out of spite because the warriors escaped before they arrived. So, to show them he meant business, he killed everybody else in the village. Lucky for Todd and Jimmy, they were left behind to guard the horses and their supplies.

Then the captain ordered the teepees and everything else they had burned to ashes. That way, when the warriors returned, there would be no homes to return to. They ran to escape the enemy, which cost their mothers, fathers, sons, and daughters their lives. Sure, Todd and Jimmy knew how evil a man the captain was. They had seen it with their own eyes. He gave them similar orders, and when they refused, he ordered the lieutenant to shoot Todd and Jimmy.

They had no choice but to shoot back. Lucky for them, the lieutenant's gun misfired, and they put a bullet into his breastplate, and took off and ran right then and there. They grabbed their horses and rode for the mountains, hoping nobody would be crazy enough to follow. They knew heading into the Rockies was risky, but what followed them was death incarnate. They had to run.

They had also seen him tell his men to rape the women and terrify the elderly. Captain Holmes always left a few wounded and frightened people behind to record history and send the word to the other tribes. He wanted the Indians to fear him. He felt he was the wrath of God, and he would eliminate all the heathens. The captain of death was riding their way. They had better get their things in order before he arrived.

Despite Hachta's begging the chief not to fight the captain, Chato thought he was trying to manipulate him out of the opportunity to beat the White captain. There would be songs made of Crow Chief Chato and not about Hachta. He had heard enough songs about him, and he was angry he was still so respected when Chato was the chief. Some of the tribe treated the war chief better than their real chief.

He knew that was because Hachta was always grandstanding with the members of the tribe in his attempt to make Chato look weak. Hachta was a large and renowned warrior who had fought over a hundred battles. He carried the scars with pride. He wore the same pride with which he had taken the scalps from Red men and White. He had never had the call to scalp a Black man, who seemed to be in a category closest to that of the Indian Nations. Since they were never hostile with the Crow and none had yet tried to settle in their mountains, they weren't considered enemies. At least not yet. Hachta had seen some Black scouts for the Army, and of course, in the war, there were many.

Hachta eyed the officer. They had taken his gun. He, too, wore the battle scars of many battles past. He was still proud in the face of ultimate defeat. Would Chief Chato best the White warrior? He had his doubts, but if he expressed more concern, the chief would take it as demeaning. So he stayed silent even though he knew the chief had chosen a dangerous path. This Indian fighter wasn't infamous without reason.

They said the number of Indians he had murdered, slaughtered, or killed was countless. At first, the captain had kept count, but when the butchery surfaced, he could no longer keep up with the numbers. To him, the count of lives didn't matter. He wouldn't be done with his mission until there wasn't an Indian left alive west of Missouri.

The Indians in eastern North America chose to trade with the White men and learn from their skills, like the Cherokee. They had many business ventures along with the Whites. They coexisted, and the Cherokee even adopted to living in log cabins for their strength and durability. But they weren't Plains Indians and didn't need to migrate to find the now-depleted herds of buffalo. In many places, like northern Texas, they had already vanished.

The chief ignored Hachta as best he could. He had to pat him on the back for his brave fight. He had gotten bruised and battered by the marshal, so he deserved no more. Now, the chief planned to show the whole tribe he was the better man and was always in line for chief. He shot a look over his shoulder, and although he was sitting straight and proud, blood flowed freely from Hachta's face.

"Now is the time for the most important battle. I, Chief Chato of the Crow Nation, will fight the Indian fighter, Captain Holmes. Bring him to the circle but search him first. Later, I will find out who is responsible for this mistake. It could have cost our war chief his life." He said the words *war chief* like he had a bad taste in his mouth.

Hachta ignored what the arrogant chief said. He was confident and knew exactly who he was while his old friend Chato had apparently forgotten. They were all boys from the same camp and grew into young men together. They had become warriors together too. Now Chato had let the position of chief taint his judgment. All the war chief could do was patiently wait and see what happened.

If evil befell the chief, he'd asked for it, and Hachta had disputed the decision for him to do so, just as he was supposed to. He was also willing to fight the captain, even though he knew he would be another creature when compared to the marshal. One was city law, and the other claimed to be the law of the plains, although the Indians disagreed with that.

All this time, Forrester sat on one side of Rusty Steel and Levi on the other. Both had their mouths open with their chins on their chests. They'd seen it when the marshal had cheated and pulled out the knife. The younger mountain men knew the marshal would win with the knife but not Rusty. He was sure no White man would easily kill a Crow war chief. He didn't have his position in the tribe because he was a creampuff.

Four warriors brought Captain Frank Holmes tied with four ropes. They were looped around his neck. They didn't do it to torture him, but it was the only way they could get him back to the fighting ring without him biting them or spitting at them.

"That man looks like a rabid dog," Levi huffed. "He don't even look like the same man."

"That's what wicked violence looks like," Rusty said

in a hushed voice. "Remember what happens here today. We're lucky we're observers. Put yourself in their place and think about what you would do and how you might fare."

When they got the captain to the center, they dropped the ropes and joined the crowd. The captain ripped the nooses off his neck and snarled at the Indians. He looked like a man who had lost his senses. His lips were pulled back from his teeth, and the veins in his neck popped. His eyes were wild like a rabid dog, and he hissed at the crowd. Still, there was no fear at all in his eyes. Captain Holmes didn't care if he didn't have any weapons. He'd grown up in the streets of a rough neighborhood and knew how to take care of himself. That and the countless battles he'd fought and massacres he had committed. The captain was well-versed in death.

For him, the chief was just another Indian. He preferred him over the war chief, who would typically be the one to take such risks. But some Indians were arrogant. Captain Holmes was quite happy to fight Chief Chato. He wasn't playing this foolish game of theirs either. He was playing for keeps. The flabby young chief wouldn't know what hit him.

Chato removed his fancy headdress and passed his knife and tomahawk to Hachta. His face was a mask chiseled of stone, and there was no telling what he was thinking. He wore the warrior face and observed detached from what happened. Chief Chato and both medicine men had decided this, so there was no disputing his participation.

"So which one of you heathen wants to come and get some first?" Captain Holmes snarled. "I can't wait to crack some skulls." He pounded his fist into his hand—you could hear it smack. His eyes were spread wide, not in fear but with the insanity of a psychopath.

Chato removed his shirt like the other warriors to show he had no weapons. Hachta was surprised at how fast the chief had let his body go. He was getting fat, and obviously, he had done nothing but eat and enjoy his new position with the tribe since he was named chief.

"So, it's going to be you, hey, creampuff?" Captain Holmes asked. "You should do me for a little warm-up before I get to that tough-looking fellow over there."

Hachta was the only Crow Indian that understood what he said. He tried to ignore what was coming, but it wasn't going to be easy.

"What did the woman killer say?" Chato asked.

"He said he would be honored to fight cha," Rusty lied, thinking quickly. "Excuse my interrupting, but I speak better English than Hachta."

The chief let it go since the mountain man had insulted his war chief. Maybe these mountain men could be valuable to Chato in ways never thought of before. He would have to remember to discuss it with them sometime when he'd sent Hachta out with a war party. He figured Hachta would be doing a lot of riding in the future. A smile escaped his lips for a fraction of a second, but Hachta, Rusty, and Captain Holmes all three saw it. It made him look devious, something Hachta had never seen, but Rusty had suspected. In the past, there was no love lost between the two.

Only Hachta stood in the way. All the tribe benefited by having steel tools and knives along with coffee and tobacco—all things they traded with Rusty and the mountain men in the compound. That was Hachta's protection. No one, not even Chato, could take that away. He might try to get between him and Rusty Steel, but Hachta knew his friend and how honorable he was. Plus, he never liked arrogant people, and Chato had always been that way, especially with him.

Chato walked toward the ring as the Crow Indians parted and made way. They all cheered their chief and champion on, confident a Crow warrior, especially a chief, could quickly beat a White man. Many of the warriors watching were becoming impatient. All these games were designed for the chief to show off. He had to beat the captain so they could torture him. They had a long, drawn-out death planned for him.

Rusty thought it was unfortunate that Marshal Wilson broke the rules and tried to kill Hachta. If he had won the fight fair and square, the outcome of his life might have changed for the better. But the path he intentionally chose sealed his fate the moment he pulled the knife out of his belt. That was when Rusty saw he was a dead man walking. For Levi and Forrester, it flew right over their heads.

Chato's mouth was a gash as his eyes narrowed. Captain Holmes rolled his fists before his face and made a few fake jabs to feel the chief out. He had no idea how to fistfight, but he planned to wrestle him to the ground. Indian wrestling was a sport they'd played ever since they were little. Beads of preparation popped up on Chato's brow. Captain Holmes's face was covered in cuts, scratches, and dirt, but those fiery eyes still blazed hatred. Why would a man hate a race of people so much?

The captain had never suffered the loss of a loved one due to the Indians. Nor had he had any member of his family or even a friend that was kidnapped by hostiles, no matter what the tribe. Nobody knew from where this hatred came. When he first came to the frontier forts, it was just another job, but for some unknown reason, it had become a crusade for the captain. He chased them and killed his new enemy with such enthusiasm that it wasn't healthy.

One person had heard Captain Holmes say that for him, it was like killing rats. They were everywhere and existed in numbers, but if a man was determined, he could kill them all. It was just a matter of persistence and not allowing others' moral codes to influence your job.

The privates sat and watched, hoping not to be noticed. Maybe they would forget about them with everything going on, and they could run out of the camp. Of course, there was a good chance they would catch them, but they didn't have much to lose. Every story they had heard of encounters with hostile Indians ended up with all the White dead. Of course, that death came after several days of torture and finally taking your scalp while still alive. They had fought real Indian warriors, and knew they were a force to be respected. It was dangerous to mess with such a hive of bees.

The sun bore down on the shirtless men, making the White men's skin red. Their arms and faces were nearly as darkly tanned as the Indians. The rest of their bodies were snow white. Todd's eyes kept darting around, looking for some way out, but there were Indians everywhere he looked. Of course, there were. They were in the middle of a Crow Indian camp. Still, there had to be a way. The possibility of them surviving without running away didn't even cross their mind, especially after the captain killed a few of theirs.

They had seen the atrocities he committed but also the violence he willingly wreaked. He was hell on wheels when fighting man-to-man, and he always led the charge. There was nothing weak or shy about this captain. To the Indian haters and those favor of their eradication, he was a hero, and many followed his exploits. Some even thought Holmes himself would kill the last of the Indian population. Never did they see such determination from a captain. He was what they needed in the frontier forts.

As soon as Chato entered the ring, to his surprise, the captain made a full-frontal attack. As he rolled his fists, it looked like he was going to punch him, so the chief prepared to dodge out of the way, but the captain faked him out and headbutted him so hard he saw stars. Holmes drew his head back and smashed it into Chato's face repeatedly. Both men's faces were covered in blood —Chato's blood.

"Come on, you're a big chief," Holmes urged him on. "I know you've got more than that. Or maybe you shouldn't be chief because you're not as hard as your people think. I believe we're about to find out, aren't we?"

The chief dropped to the ground using one leg to make a sweeping motion with his foot. Holmes's boots were kicked out from under him, and he hit the dirt hard. Now Chato smiled. He wasn't afraid of any White man. He believed they were all soft. Maybe not the mountain men from the compound but all the rest. Without their rifles and their pistols, they would be nothing.

Captain Holmes sprang back up and grinned. It actually looked like he was enjoying himself fighting an Indian. It wasn't supposed to be to the death, but Hachta didn't believe Captain Holmes could restrain himself, given the opportunity.

They sparred and exchanged contacts, but nobody got another solid punch in. Both men were patiently awaiting the perfect opportunity. There wouldn't be too many brutal clashes before one man or the other died.

Chato came in fast because he thought the captain's attention was wandering. He wasn't looking at him. He pulled a large flint stone lance head. It was much too large to use on an arrow, but still, it was a dangerous weapon in a close fight—even if it wasn't on the shaft of a lance. Hachta's face lit up like a forest fire when he saw the Crow chief cheat right in front of the entire tribe. He was appalled and so shocked at such a lack of protocol that he couldn't speak. What could he say? Tell the chief what he could or couldn't do? The tribe chief was a cheat. This brought up all kinds of questions as to their leader's honesty.

As all these thoughts bounced around in Hachta's head, Chato rushed Holmes with the spearhead, ready to thrust it into his neck. What happened next was so quick that nobody could really remember how it was after it was too late, and it was done. The warriors were not more than ten feet away. The crowd continued to push toward the center. So many people pressed forward to get a better look, it made it very hot, and the smell of sweat and fear was strong in the air.

Chato had sidestepped the captain, and before he could stop it, the captain grabbed his hand. He wrenched it back so that he wrapped his hands around the chief's and turned the knife on him. He drove it into his neck. Only the hilt was visible, and Chato gargled on his blood. The wound was mortal, and his legs immediately began to spasm, and he was gone. Captain Holmes had cut his carotid artery with his own unauthorized weapon as slick as spit.

HACHTA'S REVENGE

THE CAPTAIN'S EYES WERE CRAZED AS HE GOBBLED UP AIR to regain his composure. Blood was splattered across his face. It was the blood of Chief Chato from the cut artery in his neck. Holmes growled like a wild animal caught in a trap. Half-moons of sweat showed under his arms. All he could see was red. He sought revenge for bringing him to this point in his life. He was used to having all the power, but now he found himself nearly powerless against his foe. He thought he understood fighting and killing people, though. Now he planned to take as many heathens with him as he possibly could. They had no idea of the killing machine he was.

The captain had been fortunate, and most of his attacks in the past were against unprepared Indians. He was an expert at bushwhacking Sioux, Blackfeet, Crow, and Ute. The fact was, he had killed many more women, children, and elders than warriors. This was his first hand-to-hand combat with a hostile heathen. Of course, he'd had skirmishes with warriors on horseback, him using his saber and the Indian a tomahawk. Then, though, he'd had many men to back him up.

But standing ten feet from the man he intended to kill—the chief, no less—was new even for him. It was a strange game the Crow were playing. The captain still didn't understand the meaning of it all. He never considered that the motivating factor was honor—obviously, something that he had lost so long ago he'd forgotten it existed.

Chato was surrounded by his witch doctors, his wife, and his closest friends. Hachta used to be one of them, but Chato had shunned him as soon as he became chief. Now he was going to risk his life due to his arrogance. It was a needless waste. Hachta knew that the marshal wasn't half the man in a scrap that the captain was. He was as dangerous as a viper, and he was the worst kind of murderer. He enjoyed killing Indians, and that was a brutal fact. He had volunteered for the frontier forts so he was sure to see some action. He had been out to make a name for himself, and now he wanted the men that destroyed that dream to pay.

Hachta ordered four braves to grab the captain before he came back to his senses. He didn't know what to do. He knew the captain had to die, but how? Chato had fought and lost; if it wasn't revenged, it would stain the chief's legacy. It had already cost him his life. Still, Hachta didn't want people to think ill of him while he was in the spirit world. That was his loyalty to an old friend that had long ago changed, but still, he cared, and now, like a breath on a cold morning, he was gone in an instant.

Now that Hachta had the position of chief at his fingertips, he was undecided. He had seen what it did to his childhood friend Chato. Maybe it wasn't a good idea to be responsible for an entire camp of as many as two hundred people. In all, they had eighty warriors, so they were a force to be reckoned with, especially in the mountains.

Maybe it would be just as bad for him if he did decide to be chief—that is, if his people still wanted him. He had allowed the chief to challenge a man the war chief should have challenged. He knew he was next in line. Chato only got the honor because he married their old chief's daughter. But it was a tricky business being a war chief, too, so it must be even more so being a tribal leader and being the head of over two hundred lives. To carry such a responsibility must be a terrible burden. But who else was there to be chief, though?

It took a particular type of person just like it took a special kind of person to fight their way up the ladder to captain, major, or even general. It could be your life's goal, and when the time came, and it was finally in your grasp, you decided you didn't want it because of what it might do to a man. Power did funny things to most men, and some it destroyed—few became better men due to it.

When Hachta realized what he was thinking, he was ashamed. He knew Chato wasn't a good leader and was too absorbed with himself. Still, he had been chosen and would remain chief until he passed.

Long live Chief Chato, Hachta thought, but it sounded completely empty and void of emotion. Maybe he wasn't disappointed with his demise. The thought shocked him, but he had to stop this madness before somebody else got killed. He believed the White captain would be a dangerous man.

The fire in his eyes showed his determination, and the fact he was an Indian fighter captain must mean he was very skilled, both in combat with weapons and man-to-man. He'd already shown some of his skills to the chief. The war chief watched as his wife and family carried the body away. Just because the chief had died, this wasn't over until it was over. Every member of his tribe would challenge him if he won. Eventually, they would kill him, but still, they had to do so with honor. The chief had dishonored himself with the hidden weapon. Now, the slate had to be cleaned, and the next battle had to be fair and honorable, or this madness would never end.

Hachta stood in the circle as his sweaty body glistened in the sun. Battle scars covered his skin. The captain was similar, except his body was as white as a church. The Crow war chief's eyes were mere slits. The captain's were wild and spread wide, not in fear but in excitement. He intended to enjoy killing yet another Indian.

"Wait!" a voice called out. It was in English. "If Hachta dies, the tribe will have no leader," Levi said.

Rusty Steel looked at the young mountain man expectantly. He wanted to know what entertainment he was to provide today.

"I want to take Hachta's place," Levi said.

Johnson, the man the Indians called Beaver, unfolded his six-foot-seven frame and towered over the captain. He pulled his buckskin shirt over his head as the muscles in his chest, back, and arms rippled. He had hardened muscles made from chopping wood for the entire compound. It had made an already strong man into a monster in size and strength. A fire was there in his eyes to see, but it was still just a low boil. Soon, it would be scalding hot as his blood began to simmer.

Rusty-eyed Levi and asked, "Are ya sure you're ready for this, pilgrim? You know you'll be putting your life in danger."

"If somebody don't, the tribe might end up without a chief, and I reckon I'm as ready as I'll ever be," Levi replied. "I ain't been whooped yet, but there's always a first time."

"This won't be just a whoopin', son," Rusty replied, as serious as death. "This'll be to the end. One of ya's ain't gonna walk away. Whatcha think, Hachta? It keeps you out of this mess any more than you're already in. I doubt my boy loses anyway. This craziness has to stop here and now. This man ain't worth losing another chief over. Not in my book. Levi can take care of 'im for ya."

Levi Johnson stepped into the circle of Crow braves. Even though he knew what he was doing, it felt intimidating to have so many dangerous warriors within a few feet and all of them armed. Levi only had his bare hands, and the captain held the sharp, stone lance head in his right hand. Levi suspected he had a handful of dirt in the other.

Holmes scowled. "So I get to kill one of the Injun lovers, do I? I've never had the chance to slice up a White lowlife like you. You're a traitor to your flag and country, abetting these hostiles. If we were back in civilization, I'd have you court-martialed for treason."

"I reckon that's what you could call me—an Indian lover. I'm learnin' more from them than I'd ever learn from scum like you." Levi smiled, but his eyes told another story. He didn't seem the least bit fazed by the captain, but that didn't mean he took his eyes off him for a second. "I've got to remind ya I ain't in your army. So you have no right to tell me what I can and can't do. I'm just as White as you. I reckon we've got a bone to pick. They should call you Captain Death instead of Captain Holmes. You're the vilest person I've ever met. Every Red man in this tribe is a better person than you. It'll be my pleasure to put an end to your path of death and destruction."

Captain Holmes smiled and replied, "Thank you for the compliment. It's not every day I get to kill a White man, but I'll make an exception for you. I didn't like you from the first time you sassed me back at the cabins. I should have taught you a lesson right then and there. Better late than never, though. That's what I always say."

When he smiled, his teeth were coated in blood, making him look eviler than ever. He still had the long and sharp lance head in his right hand. He smiled a wicked smile, and it reached his eyes.

Now, the captain became the aggressor. Levi wanted to see what he had planned before he lowered the boom. He didn't intend to get stabbed in the liver and killed in the process. First, he wanted to see what the captain was really made of. That quick move with the chief didn't mean he could pull something like that off again, especially with somebody expecting a trick. The chief's ego got in his way, costing him everything he ever had and everything he would ever have. That's what happens when you lose and die. You lose everything you think you own in the blink of an eye. It just goes to prove that no matter what somebody wrote down on paper, in the end we don't really own anything.

Holmes rushed forward and jabbed twice at Levi's chest, but he blocked both thrusts. The flint blade came to within an inch of Levi's skin. They circled each other some more as Levi patiently waited to see what was in his other hand. When he saw the dirt fly, he twirled his body and used the centrifugal force to make a round-house like none he had ever made. All two hundred thirty pounds of muscle stepped into the swing.

To the captain, it all seemed to happen in slow motion. He thought he had him with his thrusts, but he blocked them with his arms an instant before the blade pierced the skin. Now he would go for the liver. The attack at the chest was a fake out, so he would expect that was his target. He knew he might not penetrate his ribcage with all that muscle, but the liver was relatively unprotected. That was his kill shot. Now he only had to wait for the moment.

That was when he saw the giant paw of a fist in his peripheral vision. It seemed to come out of nowhere, and he wasn't sure what it was at first. He watched as it seemed to grow as it neared his head. Finally, in the end, just before impact, he realized what it was. When Levi made contact, it was like the captain had been hit by a freight train.

Captain Frank Holmes heard his jaw break before he felt it. It ultimately came off its hinges and swung below his upper lip like festooned laundry on a windy day. His face imploded as Levi's fist made an impression on the side of his head that went from his teeth to above his temple. His eyes rolled back in his head, and the crowd expected him to fall. But he stood there long enough that some in the crowd thought he was impossible to put down. Finally, he fell over backward like a chopped-down tree, making a puff of dust when he landed.

Again, the warriors attacked the man they considered the villain—the man who had slaughtered their families at a whim. Somewhere back in Washington, maybe a medal was waiting for him. But this time, he would never receive the honor. It would be given posthumously. His body and the marshal's vanished, and neither Levi nor Will asked Hachta what happened to them. They were afraid to hear the answer.

Somehow, they knew Rusty Steel knew, but they were afraid to ask him too. They both realized they still had a lot to learn about Indians and the people who trespassed on their land. This had been a hard lesson, especially for Hachta.

After it was all over with the captain, the mountain men vanished just as mysteriously as they'd arrived. The privates wondered if the Crow Indians had forgotten about them. Or would they be tomorrow's distraction? Both men slept with one eye open. They knew their time was nearly up, and their fellow Americans had obviously abandoned them. They should have deserted the captain long before they had. Maybe they wouldn't have had to kill the officer. Maybe then they wouldn't have the whole Army after them. Now, a captain had died in mysterious circumstances.

Who in the world would believe them if they lived to tell the story? Maybe...a lot of things, but maybes didn't change what already was.

ESCAPE

THAT NIGHT, WHEN EVERYBODY WAS SOUND ASLEEP, Private Todd Zillow looked around wide-eyed. Paranoia was etched across his face. Jimmy Jones was stirred from his restless sleep. Their trials were over, and they had been tested for their bravery, but they didn't know what came next. Nobody had given them a sentence or told them what was happening. This fact had them at their wit's end, as fear of the unknown was the worst. It ate away at their empty stomachs. Jimmy had hurled for an hour after the captain was killed. His face was pale, and his skin clammy. He was suffering from a slight case of shock but he knew he had to buck up. It wasn't over until it was over.

With Chief Chato dead, War Chief Hachta said he would have to consider such an important decision. The tribe still didn't have a new chief. They didn't know if it would be minutes, hours, or days—maybe even weeks —before a new chief was voted in, and something was decided. As far as they knew, they may keep them for slaves if they were lucky; if not, they figured they would kill them, and they didn't expect anything but a long, drawn-out, torturous death. After what happened to Marshal Wilson and Captain Holmes, they did not expect any leniency. They would probably believe them to be as bad as the older two captives, even though their beliefs and morals reflected nothing of those of either officer of the government.

Todd nudged Jimmy, who restlessly slept beside him. He slapped his hand over his mouth before he could complain. They had to make sure nobody woke up. Jimmy's eyes locked on Todd's as they spread wide.

"Remember what Rusty Steel said about Canada?" Todd whispered. "I reckon that's just about the only chance we're gonna get. We're strong, and we still have our wits. In Canada, we won't be deserters, and maybe we can start new lives. Maybe even change our names. One thing's for sure. I'm never gonna come back to these mountains again for as long as I live—that is, if we get out."

"First, we've gotta get out of here," Jimmy replied in a hushed voice. "Iffin we're gonna go, let's go before they decide to kill or torture us. At the end of the day, we've got little to lose."

Jimmy wasn't quite as bright or quick thinking as Todd, but he instantly knew what he meant. He silently rolled up his bedroll and headed for the back of the camp. They didn't see a soul move among the Crow Indians. Some were curled up beside their fires, and others had retired to their teepees. A half-moon cast long shadows beside the fleeing soldiers. They hoped the entrance to the valley was back there like Rusty Steel had claimed. If not, they were sure to get caught by the Crow Indians. If it was there and they were lucky, they might be able to sneak away before anyone found out they were gone. They would climb back down the way they came and find the best route to Canada.

The soldiers crept along the side of the camp, hoping the Indians didn't see their silhouettes or discover they weren't in their bedrolls asleep. When they came to the canyon's end, they immediately saw the opening in the moonlight. It cast a silver glow across the landscape. Todd shot a glance over his shoulder and saw no movement. He turned back to Jimmy, and they locked eyes. Both were spread wide with fear. Then they took off in a burst of speed induced by pure adrenaline. They roared through the forest like scalded chickens.

They raced through the woods and down the hill as fast as they could run. Their hearts hammered in their heads, making it impossible to hear if they were being followed. They were too scared to shoot a glance over their shoulder. With every step, they expected an arrow in the back. After an hour, they had to slow their pace because they both had a stitch. They had pushed them-selves so hard that their breathing was ragged as they tried to gobble up as much oxygen as possible. In five minutes, they rushed off again, pushing their bodies to their limits.

Both men were acutely aware that they had no weapons or horses. At least they had warm bedrolls and suitable clothing, and plenty of fish to catch in the streams. They even had money in their leather pouches if they ever got back to civilization. They didn't know if they would make it, but at least they weren't facing torture or brutal deaths like Marshal Wilson and Captain Holmes. If the Crow did catch up with them, they would have to kill them to get them to stop. Neither private wanted to end up looking like a pincushion.

"Iffin they catch up with us, I'm gonna throw myself off a cliff before I go back to that Crow camp to be tortured," Jimmy huffed, out of breath.

"If it comes to that, I'll jump with ya, brother. It's a good thing what little money we've got is in gold coins," Todd said. "Gold spends the same everywhere."

"You don't have to talk so loud," Jimmy whispered. "Anybody could be out there listening. The folks in these mountains be as sneaky as they come."

They had been running for two hours, as hard as they could, without a stop. Finally, gasping for air, they dropped down into the grass, exhausted. They knew they had a long way to run before they could be sure they weren't being chased. Both men stood, still gasping for air with the heels of their hands on their knees. Their clothing was stuck to their backs, and their hair looked glued to their heads from sweat.

"Hush," Todd whispered. "Did you hear that?"

"Hear what?" Jimmy replied.

"I said shush, fool," Todd said as he focused on his hearing.

They only heard the animals in the night. Something rustled in the bushes behind them, and they looked back, but nothing was there. Both men were jumpy and on edge. For all they knew, sixty Crow warriors were bearing down on them. When they turned their eyes back, a big mountain man stood over them, looking down. They straightened, still gobbling air. They didn't know if he was there to take them back or kill them. Two more walked out of the shadows. They were the same mountain men present at the games and in the compound on the first day.

Both soldiers wondered what these three White men had to do with all this. They'd quietly watched as the marshal, the Indian chief, and the captain all died. They had seemed more like spectators than participants, but Todd had his doubts. He had never met a real mountain man before, and he didn't believe they would be much different than the Indians. They would probably just as soon scalp them as not, just like the warrior braves. The young soldiers believed their minutes were counted and time was ticking away.

"You were one of the mountain men who watched us go through whatever that was back in the Crow camp," Todd said. "You were the man they called Rusty. Are we safe now?"

"How do you know we ain't gonna rob ya of that gold you talked about?" Rusty grinned. He looked at the pair of soldiers with mischief in his eyes. He always seemed to be laughing at something someone had done.

"You two young morons ain't gonna make it down without a rifle and a pistol." Rusty laughed. "Considerin' you were the only two honest men of the four, we figure we owe ya somethin'. Everybody on the mountain knew you boys were here, but you never noticed a hint of our presence. You two sure as heck don't belong here in the mountains. I figure you'll be lucky to get away. Like I said before, head for Canada. If you ever tell anybody where the Crow Indian camp is, I swear I'll turn you into the law myself. Now you've got a chance to run and make a new life for yourselves. Maybe you've learned enough about life so ya don't make the same mistakes again."

"It weren't a mistake, Mr. Rusty," Todd huffed. "We was just followin' orders."

Levi Johnson passed the soldiers a brace of pistols each. Without guns, their chances of making it to Canada were nil to nothing. He gave them enough lead balls and powder to make it to Canada unless they were caught again by another war party—maybe some Black-feet Indians, who were more ruthless than the Crow.

"Oh, I reckon you made mistakes all right," the one-armed ex-captain said. "Maybe you should have requested a transfer. I was an Army man once myself, and I, too, made some bad choices, but life goes on. In the future, be more careful about who you sign on with."

Both soldiers looked at the mountain man with the empty sleeve and wondered how he had lost his arm.

"Here's some water skins, stale biscuits, and hard tack to get ya through a day or two," Rusty said as he grabbed a stick and made a map in the dirt of how they should go to make their way to Canada on a safe route. "You boys best keep in mind to stay clear of any riders— especially if they're the US Army. You'll be safe when you make it to the border, and you can start life anew."

"We brought you the marshal's and captain's horses the Crow Indians stole as soon as they hobbled them and turned their backs." Forrester's lips and eyes smiled.

"We watched the whole drama play out for a distance with my spyglass." Rusty chuckled.

"Why didn't you help us then?" Jimmy asked.

"Sometimes, it's best to let things cook a spell on

their own to know what you should or shouldn't do." Rusty laughed. His eyes were full of wit, but there was a wagonload of wisdom there too.

"Why are you helping us?" Todd asked. "Won't ya get yourselves into trouble with the Crow?"

"Do you two young men really think the Crow Indians didn't know you escaped? At least Hachta knew, just like me. We made it easy for ya to get away without letting you go in front of the whole tribe and the war chief losing face. We had to be a little sneaky. Had that fool of a marshal not tried to kill Hachta, he might have gone away free too. They just wanted to scare ya enough to make sure you'd never return to the Crow camp or tell anybody about it."

"And the captain?" Jimmy asked. "Would he have gone free too?"

"The question is, do you two think he should have gone free, or did he get what he deserved?" Rusty asked. "What do you think about it? What would you have done if you were in the Indians' shoes and had captured such a murderer? They have families just like most of us folks."

The men hesitated for a moment before they answered. They both had hated the captain, but this wasn't all that unusual for a private. They usually hated their lieutenant too. Most sergeants were close enough to the men to be tolerated. They also knew it wasn't unheard of for soldiers to shoot their officers when they sent them ahead as cannon fodder. But were they prepared to ignore their sins against the Almighty just like most soldiers they'd met on the Indian frontiers?

When the captain's orders came to them via the lieutenant, they didn't have the stomach to kill innocent people. The privates weren't like the captain and didn't believe the Indians were simply animals. They were real people which the Army believed should be eliminated as quickly as possible so their progress and civilization machines could run them over with the least resistance. These people were the warriors' parents, children, and wives. They weren't Todd and Jimmy's enemies.

They never bore arms against either man. They understood their orders when they were told to fight war parties. Sometimes they ambushed the soldiers. But the attacks on the villages when the warriors were out hunting or maybe even fighting Whites, they couldn't rationalize. These acts were clearly against their own moral values. Apparently, their lieutenant and captain had none.

"Are you sure the Crow warriors ain't gonna come and chase us down?" Jimmy asked. He brushed his black hair out of his charcoal eyes. "I doubt we be a match for them even armed with a couple of pistols."

Hachta stepped out of the shadows. The blood drained from the soldiers' faces, and Rusty laughed. The Crow war chief had been there the whole time and listened to everything. Steel loved a good show as he saw life as one enormous folly. He and the war chief had worked out the plan. It was a way for two innocent men to escape a certain death without Hachta losing face in front of the tribe. When the war chief came out of the dark, they saw he was painted for war, and their hearts dropped. Maybe they were going to die anyway.

They both thought the jig was up. Maybe the mountain men were in cahoots with the hostiles. They sure were friendly enough back in their stronghold. Todd wondered if these mountain men were half Indian, part animal, or maybe a mix of both. They didn't act like any White men they had ever met. They even dressed like Indians.

"You should get rid of your horses as soon as ya can. Your duds, too," Rusty said. "That don't mean steal a couple of horses or rob somebody's clothesline either. Use those gold coins you were blabberin' about to buy some and keep your voice down when you talk about valuables up here—or anywhere west of the Missouri River. If almost anybody but us hears you talk about money, you stand a good chance of getting robbed. Stay off the main trails and use the secondary routes. You won't be spotted as quickly."

"So, why are you lettin' us go?" Todd said. "We're deserters."

"You ain't deserters," Hachta replied. "You are smart, honest men, is all. Nobody should be told to kill women and children, no matter who gave the orders."

"So, you're really lettin' us go, Chief?" Jimmy asked as he blinked his eyes. A single tear cut a path down his dust-covered face. It was a sincere sign of gratitude.

Suddenly, the chief shot his blazing eyes toward the soldiers. They weren't kind, and the smile turned into a frown.

"If I see either of you again, anywhere, I will kill you both," Hachta said in a deadly voice. "This time the threat of torture won't be hollow. This is the last warning you will get from the Crow Indians. You are to leave the mountains at once. Maybe you will be lucky and won't catch the first fall snow. My people are all in mourning for the loss of our chief. No one will follow you for some days, but I can't guarantee what my warriors will do after that. An Indian war chief never has complete control over his men.

"Much like your captain didn't have control of you two. Men do things they feel they have to at times, and others won't ever understand why they did it."

THE PORCH

EIGHT MOUNTAIN MEN SAT ON RUSTY STEEL'S PORCH. IT was early morning and the first cold day of an early fall in the Rockies. A prism of rays shot across the sky with the morning sunrise. The last stars in the west were just disappearing. It was Will Forrester's turn to do the honors and cook breakfast, and he was making a mess of the fried eggs. The men ordered their eggs sunny side up, but he broke every yolk. Seven hungry men sat on the porch in bear and buffalo skin coats; some were already wearing their fur-lined moccasins. Breaths of steam came from the grumpy men waiting on their coffees. This was one time when patience went right out the window.

"I must say," Angus said, "there was a wagonload of learning y'all did back there. If it had only been Rusty here tellin' the tale, I reckon I'd only believe half, but with Levi Johnson and Forrester there too, I can't doubt a word, now can I?"

"Are you callin' me a liar?" Rusty barked. "And where's my coffee, you old fool?"

"Don't look at me. It's not my turn." Angus cackled like an old hen.

"Do you think Todd and Jimmy will make it to Canada?" Levi Johnson asked. He was worried about the two confused soldiers. "I reckon those two should never have been soldiers in the first place."

"And it's a danged good thing for them." Rusty laughed. "Had they put up a good enough scrap to kill one of the warriors, I doubt they'd be alive today."

"You still didn't answer my question," Levi retorted.

"I know the real Army won't go looking for them before the snow melts in the spring," Forrester said. "But then they'll come as sure as we're sitting here. That is, if they can figure out where they went."

"Every bounty hunter I've had the misfortune to meet keeps tight lips about where his next bounty is," Dennis observed. "It's obvious they've gotta keep it a secret until they catch or kill 'im."

"Come on, Rusty," Levi grumbled. "What are the odds those two young soldiers make it to Canada?"

"I figure if they don't go off the trail I showed 'em, they'll make it sure enough. That is, iffin they don't run into a bunch of Blackfeet Indians first." Rusty chuckled. "They ain't nearly as friendly as the Crow. Why, if we built a cabin on Blackfoot land, we'd be dead in a week. The Crow Indians are a little cleverer and know they need White men to trade their furs and pelts. That's what keeps us safe up here. It ain't because Dennis and I are pretty."

"I don't believe that for a minute," ex-Captain Will Forrester said. "I saw the respect the tribe had for you, Rusty. They hardly gave us a second glance."

"Maybe at first they just put up with your ugly faces

and Rusty's nasty disposition to trade for White men's tools." Levi laughed. "I figure you slowly grew on 'em just like you did with us. You didn't treat us much better when we first met. You take a spell to side up to a man."

"The Crow treat us good because we treat them like we treat each other. With a boatload of respect." Rusty smiled, and it reached his eyes.

Despite his gruff nature and the fact Rusty saw life as one enormous folly, he had a soft spot in his heart for these two young mountain men. They would be his legacy when he passed on to the other side, but he knew he had a ton of work to do before then. They still had more to learn than they could ever imagine.

"Well, now that everything's safe again, I'm gonna go home to my wife for a week or two." Angus grinned like a possum. "Maybe I'll bring Green Leaves back with me. I hope things have settled down in the stronghold. But then again, I've never been a threat to the local Indians. They think I'm special because I dance so well. I reckon it's because the Indians put so much stock in dancin'. Ain't it funny how all women like a man who can cut up a rug and leave 'em spellbound? Then they're like butter in my hands."

Rusty just shook his head, and Dennis laughed. Angus seemed so ugly to them a mirror would turn him away. But to the Crow women, he was a prize catch. All eight men were roaring in seconds, but it was a nervous laughter. Even those who had stayed back in the compound knew that if things had gone wrong, they would all be in a mess right now. They were lucky to have both Angus and Rusty as their ambassadors with the Crow Indians. Of course, that wouldn't guarantee a future free of problems. Even the Indians had to battle Mother Nature in the wilderness.

Hopefully, this peace would last. Then again, the world was changing so fast that none expected things to stay the same for too much longer. All this may well be changed in ten short years, and not for the better. From here on out, things could only get worse, with the shortage of wild game and buffalo, and an excess of White folks.

God reeled the sun higher into the sky until its rays warmed their faces. All eight mountain men turned toward the glowing orb. Smiles stretched across their lips like the Rocky Mountains stretch from Canada to New Mexico. There was not another place in the whole world they would rather be and no other friends they would like to share the glory of Mother Nature with. The older six mountain men's hair was graying as age advanced on its unstoppable course. The two newcomers blew some new life into their compound, making life more attractive again as they saw everything anew through Levi and Forrester's eyes.

Sure, Rusty, Dennis, Angus, and even Sam, Bob, and Pete had a great deal to do with the success of teaching the two newcomers the ways of the wilderness. Strangely enough, they benefited just as much as Levi and Forrester. The curious young men gave a new meaning to life and provided endless entertainment, one of the things that Rusty looked for in a friend.

A Look at Book Four:
Brotherhood: A Western Double

Among the snow-capped peaks, brotherhood is tempered by grit and survival.

Brotherhood

Levi Johnson and former army Captain Will Forrester push deep into the Rockies, trapping beaver as the first snow blankets the mountains. With their mules loaded high with prime pelts, they return to the compound eager to prove themselves to their new companions. A busy winter lies ahead —if the wilderness doesn't claim them first.

But the arrival of a lone US Cavalry major riding in uninvited stirs unease among the mountain men. He comes searching for someone, but his bold intrusion could bring more than just questions—sparking tension among the mountain men and hints at trouble that won't be easily left behind.

Journeys

When the Crow claim the best trapping grounds as their own, Levi and Will set out again—despite warnings that the mountain storms show no mercy. They find untouched springs and a fortune in pelts, but they're not alone. A ruthless gang of scalpers stalks them through the trees, watching, waiting to take both hides and lives.

When Levi discovers a captive Crow warrior woman among the thieves, he knows he must risk everything to save her— even if it means fighting killers in a frozen land where every step could be their last.

AVAILABLE AUGUST 2025

ABOUT THE AUTHOR

Ash Lingam was born and raised in Southern Ohio, not far from the mighty Ohio River. He had somewhat of an isolated upbringing on a family farm with his sisters. His best friends were his horse, Sugar, and his grandfather.

Born in 1886, the family patriarch grew crops, raised cattle, and doted on the young boy. At his grandfather's side, Ash learned about livestock and firearms at an early age. His grandad carried an old Colt with him at all times. It helped spawn a young boy's dreams of yesteryear.

Ash was only eight years old when his grandad taught him how to trap muskrats to prevent them from draining the farm's ponds. He gave him a double-barreled shotgun at twelve and taught him how to hunt to put food on the table.

It wasn't long before Ash was breaking horses. His spirited Tennessee Walker never allowed any other rider on her back. Together, they searched through the plowed fields in the spring, looking for Miami Indian arrowheads to add to his grandfather's ample collection.

Ash's family was among the early settlers in pre-

Revolutionary America. He has traced his lineage back to around 1746 when his ancestors immigrated from Europe to the aspiring American Colonies.

A retired marketing executive, Ash devotes his spare time to training police dogs and writing novels. He has found his niche in the Western, historical fiction, and adventure genres. With his vast vault of experience, he never runs out of sources for new stories. He has lived in eleven different countries and worked in a total of forty-six to date, Ash has written approximately 130 novels, short stories, and poems. More than one hundred of his eclectic titles help the American frontier come alive for his readers.

https://www.ashlingam.com/
Join the Lawless Waters Western Readers & Writers
Facebook Group